The
Miniature Man

r muir

snowbooks

Special promotional edition

Proudly published by

Snowbooks Ltd.

120 Pentonville Road

London

N1 9JN

Tel: 0207 837 6482

Fax: 0207 837 6348

email: info@snowbooks.com

www.snowbooks.com

British Library Cataloguing in Publication Data

A catalogue record for this book is available from the British Library.

ISBN 1-905005-52-0

ISBN13: 978-1905005-52-9

Printed and bound in Great Britain

The Miniature Man

r. muir

PROLOGUE

The cicadas screamed. Their shrill, interminable cry gnawed into the girl's brain like acid. She lay on her side, her knees drawn up toward her chest against the pain. Her flesh was torn and raw and now unpityingly scorched on that side exposed to the caustic desert sun. But though her body sweltered, and the stones beneath it stabbed like broken glass, she could not move.

"Don't hurt me anymore." "Don't hurt me anymore." The phrase droned over and over in her mind as if the tape across her mouth had locked it in. "Don't hurt me anymore;" its rhythm strangely mimicked by the flashing red/blue lights that suddenly appeared as if to mock her

3

helplessness with alternating stares.

'Oh, my good God!'

'Is she alive?'

'Barely. Get a blanket from the car, will ya? And call the Rescue Unit.'

While the one officer hurried back, the other tried to shield the girl from the midday sun.

'Don't worry, honey. You're gonna be okay.'

He had to force back the rage and nausea that swept over him on seeing the gore. The girl was naked, bloodied, had been gagged and bound with heavy tape, beaten, evidently raped, and mercilessly left alone to die. All the hair had been shaved from her body. Both eyes were blackened and swollen shut.

'They're on their way. Shouldn't we at least un-tape her hands and feet?'

'No, we'd have to move her.' He covered the blistered body with the blanket. 'There's an awful lot of blood between her legs. And she's been burned.'

'Jesus, she's just a kid. Whataya think? Fourteen? Fifteen?'

'Better take a look around.'

More flashing lights appeared. The medics worked quickly, efficiently. Before long the girl's bonds were cut, the gag peeled off, and she was gingerly lifted onto a stretcher—I.V. and blood-transfusion bottles dangling over her bald and battered, oxygen-masked head. They carried her into the waiting van.

'Hey, is she gonna make it?'

The driver closed the double doors and turned to the officer.

'Maybe.'

'Did she say anything?'

'Yeah. "Don't hurt me anymore."'

'Jesus Christ.'

The ambulance pulled away. The patrol car followed.

On the ground where the girl had lain remained a pool of clotted blood, as though the earth itself had ruptured. The sun glared down to cauterize the wound. The cicadas screamed.

MARCY

My name is Marcy. I don't know how I got here but here I am. I don't know how long I've been here. There are a lot of things I don't know. Even my name—Marcy. I'm not sure that's right. The nuns call me that but I really don't remember. I guess that's why I'm here—I don't remember things. It's real odd. I mean to be grown up, or almost grown up, and not be able to remember how you got that way.

But Sister Zoë says I have to try. That's why she gave me this pen and paper. I like the paper. It's bound like in a book. The pen leaks a little. I'm supposed to write down anything I remember, anytime, anywhere. And it can all stay private if I want. Sister was definite about that. I don't even have to show her if I don't want.

The thing is, so far, I haven't been able to think. And I'm trying, too. Just nothing comes.

On June 6th, Marcy had been admitted to Good Samaritan Hospital with severe concussion, lacerated hymen, anterior laceration of rectal mucosa, three dislocated fingers, multiple cuts and contusions, and sixteen cigarette burns on her breasts and buttocks. She was suffering from exposure, stupor, global amnesia, and was later found to have contracted syphilis as a result of the assault. She was not impregnated.

In the weeks that followed, the authorities were able to uncover more information about her attackers than about their victim. The identities of none, however, had come to light.

On September 2nd, Marcy was declared a Ward of the State and transferred to St. Francis Sanitarium for rest and psychiatric care. The name "Marcy" was arbitrarily given her pending positive identification. She was approximately fourteen years old, 5 feet 2 inches tall, 102 pounds, brown eyes and brows, left-handed.

I'm scared. Today I found this pen and paper and one page with some writing on it. It's mine. But I had completely forgotten until I read it. I told Sister about this and she says she gave me the paper four days ago, and not to worry, just keep trying. From now on I'm going to write every day and especially put down the date, even the time. It's Tuesday, September 16th, at ten o'clock in the A.M. I have everything laid out on the table next to my bed now, so I'll be sure to see it in the morning. I won't bother writing anymore until tomorrow.

'How do you feel today, Marcy?'

'Fine.'

'I thought we'd have another little chat, if you don't mind.'

'No, I don't mind.'

'Do you want to sit, or would you like to lie down?'

'Sit.'

'Shall we sit together then?'

The elderly nun came from behind her desk and sat on the sofa, offering Marcy a place beside her. The girl sat down.

'May I hold your hand?'

Marcy hesitated. Her fingers reflexively clenched.

'That's all right. It's always up to you, Marcy. I'll never try to make you do anything you don't want to do. Are you comfortable?'

Her fists relaxed a little. The multitude of wrinkles that defined the Sister's wimpled face seemed kindly.

'Uh huh.'

'Well, take a minute and get really comfortable because, very shortly, I'm going to ask you to go to sleep.'

'But I'm not even tired.'

'This is a different type of sleep. You can do this kind with your eyes wide open; though it's usually more pleasant to keep them shut.'

'Like hypnosis?'

'Exactly.'

Marcy shifted around on the couch, took a pillow from the corner, placed it over her lap, then folded her hands atop it neatly.

'Okay, I'm ready.'

'Let's begin then by taking three deep breaths. If you use your stomach muscles first and then your chest muscles, you can take in a lot more air… That's it… In through your nose, out through your mouth. Nice and slow and steady… Good… Now try to picture a little door in the center of your forehead. It may be easier if you close your eyes. The door is rounded at the top, and as I speak it's slowly opening. Inside you can feel a warm, soft light glowing… Pretend now you're walking there, through the archway… finding yourself on the top step of a beautiful spiral staircase that winds in graceful turns all the way down your spine. There is a railing for safety that you can touch with your hand. Do you feel it?'

'Sort of.'

'Good. Now, at your own pace, I'd like you to start down the stairs, imagining that your spine is becoming more and more relaxed with every turn. Ready?'

'Yes.'

'Begin… Take your time… Breathe easily… Let all the tension disappear… Turning… Turning… Down… Down… Down… When you reach the bottom there will be a pair of doors with a button on the wall beside them… Are you there yet?'

'Uh huh.'

'Press it, and when the doors open you'll see it's an elevator with a thick carpet on the floor and a picture window on the opposite side. It's well lighted and very safe… Are you inside?'

'Yes.'

'Good. Now as the doors close you'll see two more buttons. One says "up", the other "down". When you're ready, push the "down" button, then face the window and watch the number on the wall outside. The first one is one hundred. Tell me when you're moving.'

'Now.'

'Watch the numbers. Ninety-nine… Ninety-eight… Ninety-seven… They're passing at a slow, comfortable speed… Ninety-four… Ninety-three… Ninety-two… Ninety-one…'

At "fifty", Sister Zoë suggested that the elevator pause.

'Are you still feeling relaxed and at ease, Marcy?'

'Yes.'

'If you look above you, you'll see that the ceiling, too, has a window through which you can look. Way, way up

10

at the very top you can see where we began. See?'

'Yes.'

'Now, as we go deeper, whatever sounds you hear around you will gradually grow faint and finally disappear. The only one you'll still be able to hear is the sound of my voice. Are you ready?'

'Yes.'

'Press the button… and down we go. Forty-nine… Forty-eight… Forty-seven… The sounds are fading away… and as we go deeper your eyelids are beginning to feel very heavy. It feels good, in fact, that your eyes are already closed because they're wonderfully, wonderfully tired. It would almost be too hard to open them… much more pleasant to leave them closed… relaxed… almost sleeping… relaxed… and sound… sound… asleep.

'Can you hear me, Marcy?'

'Yes.'

'Do you know where you are?'

'Elevator.'

'That's right. You're in your own private elevator and in just a moment the doors are going to open and you'll step out into a very special room that's full of familiar things… things only you can know… things only you can describe… Get ready; the doors are opening… You're stepping out… Now tell me what you see.'

The room was dark at first and smelled of mildew, dust, and time. But as her eyes adjusted to the light, its contents materialized. There were books galore—cloth-bound, leather-bound—stacks piled high; on shelves, under tables, all up and down the musty walls. They seemed to be the building blocks from which the room was made, and formed a labyrinthine scheme of dusky passageways, through which, with modest trepidation, Marcy bravely crept.

'Books.'

'You see books, Marcy? What kind?'

'All kinds. Old.'

The avenues between the books grew tall and very narrow, some barely wide enough to wriggle through. Here and there, wherever books were missing from the shelves, gaped pitch-dark pockets. Another turn; more shadows stared—pockets swelled to giant size, black, suspicious, secretive. Marcy's courage, in reverse proportion, seemed to wane. She tried to keep her eyes from glancing to the left or right while passing, but her focus, in spite of her fervent efforts, strayed. She froze in her tracks.

Worlds! The inner walls were honeycombed with precious miniature worlds! Fascinated, she peered at one after another: castles, villas, and stately mansions, farms, a forest, a volcanic isle—each created with such meticulous detail, they almost could pass for real.

'Marcy?'

The corridors were widening and on the ceiling, farther in, a light reflected from an unseen source below.

Marcy's heartbeats quickened. She sensed that from this inmost sanctum a nameless danger loomed, yet something drew her on—an intuition that she would be protected. The light was brighter, the turns more frequent, the lifelike settings fewer. Then, as she rounded one last corner, there he was.

'A man!'

'What man? Can you describe him?… Marcy?… Marcy?'

He sat amid a chaotic mass of wood and glue and glass and paint, fabric scraps, mounds of clay, plaster, paste, papier-mâché, wax and string, spools of thread, ink, balloons, coloring crayons, bits of yarn, fur and hair, needles, chisels, hammers, nails, tweezers, toothpicks, tacks and staples, and so much more the man seemed nearly buried underneath.

Looking up from his work, he peremptorily motioned Marcy in. She ventured forward, drawn less by the old man's manner than by his weird gargantuan eye. It looked both odd and terrible, magnified as it was by the thick monocle he wore on a strap around his head. She took a minute getting used to the sight—orbs of such unequal size that stared at her and blinked three times, then unceremoniously closed.

She noticed then his hands—wonderful hands. Like gnarled wood they flexed with a rough-hewn grace— knuckles for knots, veins as roots, the wrinkles deep in simulated grain. They held a piece of ivory from which was carved a tiny man, held it as if offering it to her.

Marcy stared amazed, so perfect were its features. Had she failed to see that the hands that held it trembled slightly, she surely would have sworn the figure breathed.

'May I hold him?'

The mismatched eyes shot open.

Don't talk so loud!

She started.

'I'm sorry.'

'What, Marcy? I didn't hear.'

You've done it again!

'But…'

Too loud! If you want to stay, you'll have to behave. There's no need to shout just because I'm an old man. I'm not hard-of-hearing, you know.

Confused, Marcy tried again in her softest whisper.

'Is this all…'

NO! I told you I'm not deaf.

Thoroughly flustered, Marcy tried moving her lips without uttering a sound, mouthing another apology.

I'm sorry.

That's better. A bit grotesque, scrunching your mouth up that way, but better.

He modified his tone.

I'm not angry, mind you. You'd know if I were angry. Really riled I'm a terrible sight—hair standing up on end, eyes bugged out, cheeks puffed, nostrils flaring. Just terrible. You wouldn't like it. I don't like it. Glad you caught on as fast as you did.

Marcy was about to speak again but thought better of it.

Now, about this visit you've decided to pay me. I know pretty much why you've come, even if you don't.

He interrupted himself to pour a cup of steaming coffee from a pot that sat over a hot plate on his workbench.

Want some? No? It'll put hair on your chest. Or rather on your noodle.

Huh?

Never mind. All in good time. All in good time.

He took a long, loud slurp (his monocle fogging) and sighed.

Ahhhhh, Ethiopian. Marvelous stuff. Now, to the issue

at hand—before what's-her-name gets fidgety and calls you back. This little man you've so admired is for you.

He placed it in her palm.

Don't expect to keep him though. He's going to disappear for a while as soon as you leave here anyway. Just the same, it's best you know right now; he's not to be thought of possessively. Ruins things. Always has, always will. Try to think of him instead as somebody well worth knowing. A friend. That'll be far better in the long run.

'Marcy?'

Drat. Time. When you're enjoying yourself it winks right by; when things are awful it lumbers on forever.

As if to assure Marcy of the category into which she fit, he winked at her.

Think you can find your way out?

I don't know. I think so.

And back again?

I'd like that, yes. I'll try. Thank you.

Then good-bye.

Abruptly he returned to his work. A bit nonplussed, Marcy squeezed the little figure in her hand and, as she turned, was magically back at the elevator doors.

'Marcy?... Marcy?'

'Yes?'

'You're walking back to the elevator now. The doors are opening. You're stepping inside... Are you there?'

'Yes.'

'Good. Now listen carefully. The next time we use your elevator we'll be able to go up and down much faster. In a moment you'll push the "up" button. When you do you'll move quickly up to floor one hundred and to wakefulness. You'll feel fresh and rested and wide awake. And you will remember everything you have seen, heard, smelled, touched, even tasted. Do you understand?'

'Yes.'

'Then push the button, and up we go... Ten... Twenty... Thirty... Forty... Fifty... Sixty... Seventy... Eighty... Ninety... One hundred.'

* * *

It's Wednesday, September 17th, at 9:03 in the A.M. Yesterday I got hypnotized! Sister Zoë did it. And when I was under I met the Miniature Man. He was gruff and hollered at me and made me talk without making a single sound, but even so, I liked him. I think he liked me, too. I say that because before I had to leave he gave me a present. That's the part I didn't tell Sister. I would have if I'd had the proof but when I opened my eyes to be awake, the present—a tiny little ivory man—was gone. The funny thing is, he warned me that would happen. I just didn't believe him. I had it tight in my hand. I know I didn't drop it. There's no sense writing down the rest that happened because I told it all after. What's important is that I still remember.

Sister Dana stood anxiously outside Sister Zoë's quarters waiting for the chapel bell to toll ten, the hour of her appointment. It had been her task to care for Marcy during her convalescence but, due to an incident now three days old, she felt she had failed miserably.

She had mostly ministered to Marcy's physical needs, for when admitted, Marcy still suffered from periodic stupor. Days would sometimes pass during which she would function rather dully—with Sister Dana faithfully attending her. The passive character of these states afforded the nun an easy routine that, once established, quickly lulled her into taking certain things for granted. One of these was Marcy's indifference toward being touched. She had shown, in fact, no sign whatever of feeling the hands of those who nursed her—until, that is, on the occasion of her first full bath.

Sister Dana had run the water, undressed the girl, helped her into the tub, and was tenderly soaping Marcy's body when, without warning, Marcy shrieked. It brought staff running from all directions. They burst in, Sister Zoë among them. Sister Dana—embarrassed and mortified—fled the room; which had made, she believed in retrospect, an even worse impression.

The subsequent guilt with which she tortured herself was caused in part by the circumstances of having had a patient in her care emotionally explode. But another part was attributable to the young nun's secret fears that something in her manner while bathing Marcy had set off the tantrum. And how humiliating that Sister Zoë had seen!

The door before her opened.

'Ah, there you are, Sister Dana. Come in. I've made us a pot of tea.'

Struggling to conceal her agitation, Sister Dana entered.

Despite Sister Zoë's authority and high position in their Order, little distinguished her quarters from the other Sisters'. The room was simple: wooden floors, white stucco walls mostly unadorned, a window. What furnishings there were bespoke utility. And yet there was a difference—a sort of feel more than anything overt, a sense of integrity that made the sparseness rich by virtue of its pure intentions. Sister Zoë knew who she was and what her role in life should be. The strength of those convictions stood out around her.

'Please, sit down. I thought our chat would be more pleasant here. Cream?'

'Yes, please.'

'Sugar?'

'Two.'

'You're looking tired. Are you not sleeping well?'

'Not very, Sister, no.'

'You should try a cup of warm milk before retiring. I know it's an old-wives'-tale remedy, but that hasn't made it any less effective through the years.'

'Thank you, Sister, I will.'

They sipped their tea. Under the wise, insightful eyes of her superior, Sister Dana felt comforted—but also threatened. In troubles past, the senior nun had always offered prudent counsel. But this was different.

'Now, about what did you wish to see me?'

'You know. You must.'

'Marcy.'

'I'll never forgive myself for the way I acted, Sister.'

'Your being upset was quite understandable; the whole place was in a dither after Marcy's awful scream.'

'But running away like I did…'

'Was unprofessional, yes. I trust you'll muster more control in the future.'

'Yes. Oh, yes, Sister, I will. I don't know what came

over me.'

'Was there anything else?'

'Else?'

'About which you wanted to see me.'

'Well… no. Only that I'm terribly sorry.'

She was amazed that Sister Zoë appeared so ready to dismiss the matter.

'Apology accepted.'

Much relieved, Sister Dana rose to go.

'But there are some other things I'd like to discuss with you.'

She sat back down.

'Some recent developments in Marcy's case. I thought you ought to know for our work ahead.'

'"Our work"? You mean you still want me to care for her?'

'In an adjusted capacity, yes.'

'But what about what happened?'

'Oh, I'm sure she's forgotten that already. Whatever it was is locked back up with the bulk of Marcy's secrets. Lucky for us we caught at least a glimpse of what may be a key.'

'I don't understand.'

'Intimate contact.'

For the remainder of the interview, Sister Zoë related her observations about the success and, more significantly, the failure of her hypnotherapy. Of particular concern was Marcy's disregard for some of the suggestions. Her feedback showed (contrary to the preconditions) that there was nothing familiar about the room that she had visited. Having anticipated that the trance state would expose Marcy's untold past, this turn of events mystified the nun. Furthermore, such errant jaunts were dangerous, for though the girl reported later that she had been in no real danger, the fact remained that for a time she had strayed beyond her therapist's control. Perhaps hypnosis was not the best tool for unearthing Marcy's memory.

'Must she remember, Sister Zoë?'

'Yes, I'm afraid she must. No matter how deeply her past is buried, it's bound to resurface. If that can happen while help is near, her psyche may survive it. But alone, I fear, Marcy's memories could prove quite unendurable.'

After Sister Dana left, her plaintive question echoed—
Must she remember, Sister Zoë?

Must she? The nun closed her eyes and wondered what God's plan for such a one might be.

JULIAN

Pawn to King four. The opening move had been made, the time clock begun, and still only one man sat at the center-stage table. Had it not been for the repeated supplications by the tournament host, the match would have been forfeited.

The Grandmaster shifted irritably in his chair. It was an affront, he felt, unforgivable under the circumstances. For this, in fact, was not a tournament but an exhibition. He wished now he had declined the invitation. After all, what was there to gain? He checked the time, casting another impatient look at the nervous referee. This brand of theatrical "one-upmanship" was insolent, regardless of the upstart's reputation.

Yet the indignity of waiting for an unranked player, before a small but astute audience of chess enthusiasts, was not his prime vexation, for underscoring the Master's pique was a latent apprehensiveness about the match's outcome. His unpunctual opponent—a boy, a prodigy—had played eleven top-ranked players to date and beaten them all. The games were unofficial; the U.S. Chess Federation had no record of them. But their contents, replete with unique positions and radical lines of play, were, nonetheless, being analyzed in clubs across the country. Julian Papp was well-known. So much so that to refuse his challenge and keep one's credibility intact was becoming progressively harder.

The seconds ticked off. Perhaps the boy would be a no-show. From past accounts, arriving late was not among his characteristics. Concentration, uncanny skill, innovative moves—these traits were invariably cited—but tardiness, never. The crowd was already anxious. These exhibitions had brought prestige to their otherwise unheralded club. Julian Papp—sobriquet The Albino—had become their standard-bearer. Annihilating the local competition at the age of twelve, he had been awarded the honor of playing a visiting Grandmaster.

He had won!

In a similar match the following year, his victory was repeated, and thus the legend began. But his remained a strictly word-of-mouth fame, for when Julian was invited to compete in the more publicized major tournaments he declined, announcing that he would participate solely in exhibition play, and this only locally. Then, with a self-assured arrogance reminiscent of Paul Morphy, he issued an open challenge to any Grandmaster who was willing to meet him on home ground. Much to the delight of his chess club, the challenge was sometimes accepted—at first rather lightly by visiting Masters curious about the boy's talent, then later, as his winning record became nationally known, in earnest.

By tradition a single game was played. The challenger chose for White or Black. A draw precipitated a second game. Three draws and Julian conceded defeat—a concession he had never made during his entire eight years of competitive play.

Relief nuzzled into the Grandmaster's fidgety nerves. Time was running out. Failure to appear was admission of defeat, and though this was hardly the most satisfying means by which to achieve a win, certain statements by the vanquished implied it might be preferable to running the risk of losing. For rumored more indomitable than his caliber of play was the young man's eerie mien across the board. Its effect had been expressed in terms like "intimidating" and "unnerving"—and by those unused to being flustered. Whether this indeed was true, or merely the rationalization of wounded vanities, was perhaps a matter that should best be left untested.

The thirty-minute grace period was almost up. Beyond that, waiting out the hour was at the discretion of the player present. Judging by the huffy agitation in the Master's manner, it was unlikely he would prove to be magnanimous.

The audience stirred. At the side of the hall a door opened. With a steady, unhurried step, Mr. Julian Papp entered. He wore white; he was white: white sneakers, socks, pants, suspenders, long-sleeve shirt and tie, white hair, white skin—a pasty shade of corpselike pallor. In fact his skin color seemed to have no depth, but lay on the surface like an opaque mask: anemic, static, inhumanly expressionless. It was easier to keep one's face averted, for if one did brave a surreptitious glance, it was apprehended, caught and swallowed up by the case-hardened blue-black lenses that enshrouded the chess player's eyes. Invariably they drew focus—like twin black holes.

Having mounted the stage and crossed to his seat, Julian imperceptibly nodded, sat, and immediately answered the opening move with Pawn to Queen Bishop's four. The clock was punched, the tone established. Total silence reigned.

Stiffening in his chair, the Grandmaster sucked in his disgruntlement and directed his gaze toward the sun-shielded eyes of the anomalous Julian Papp—whose dark glasses proved impenetrable. Discomfiture suddenly threatening, the Grandmaster's scrutiny returned to the board. He deliberated long and hard:

2. Nf3

Instantly Julian answered:

2.........e6

Thus the pattern of play was set. Every plodding move by the Master was to receive a lightning reply. It was an effective tactic, particularly in combination with Julian's remarkable appearance—which his opponent seemed determined to ignore.

3. d4

3.........cxd4

The pawn was snatched with a startling covetousness. It was as if the boy in white were reclaiming a portion of himself. His moves were reflexes. Then, after each, he returned to a cataleptic calm.

The match continued. For the benefit of the spectators, each move was reproduced on a video screen erected at the back of the stage. On move twenty-four the Grandmaster blundered. Awareness of this, like an electric shock, went rippling through the crowd. Julian's retort was instantaneous, implacable. And though the game was far from lost, White's position was seriously weakened.

Then a change came over Julian, a subtle movement. With his hands resting on either chair arm, his thumbs commenced to beat an irregular time.

wind breathing soft gentle meadowscents and

meadowcolors walking (touch me touch me) passing through the air molecules of air pulsebeat footfall time adrift (she) yes (touch me hold my hand) the meadow smiling as we walking floating reaching touch to touching palm to palm two palm prints pressing lines whose fates conjoined inscribe the way so clear so clear so clear

It lasted only seconds, then it stopped. Those familiar with Julian's play recognized the motion. He had always done it. This seemingly involuntary tapping was popularly thought to be triggered by fluctuations in the mental rigors exacted by the game. It was not, however, a reliable barometer of how a given match was going, for as often as not the thumbs started up without anything overt happening. And since Julian himself offered no explanation, his fans simply shrugged off the quirk, as they did so many of their champion's idiosyncrasies.

By the fortieth move, White's earlier mistake was beginning to take its toll. Julian had kept up his high-pressure pace and also—more than ever before—his interludes of tapping. Increasingly aware of the precariousness of his position, the Grandmaster seized on the inaudible thumbs as the cause of his predicament. When next they resumed—at move forty-two—he complained to the referee.

'Would you kindly ask my opponent to desist from that interminable pounding?'

With White's position nearly hopeless, the referee was

not surprised, believing, as did all those present, that the Master should resign. Nonetheless, he obliged.

'Mr. Papp?… Mr. Papp?'

the air   molecules of air   pulsebeat time adrift (she) yes (touch me hold my hand) the meadow smiling…

yes (touch me hold my hand) the meadow…

the meadow…

the meadow!

The twitching in his thumbs crept up his arms. His shoulders quaked, as did his head, his legs. He clenched the chair as if to squelch the tremors. Suddenly a birdlike cry erupted from his lungs.

'Mr. Papp!'

A violent spasm sent Julian rocking. His chair tilted back. It balanced nervously on end for a second, wavered, then crashed to the floor. Crowd members rushed to the stage.

'Loosen his clothing!'

'Take off his shoes!'

Julian's face had turned blue.

'Stick something between his teeth!'

He seemed to be gagging.

'Watch that he doesn't swallow his tongue!'

His chest heaved for air.

'Give him some room. Back up. Everybody back up!'

'Shouldn't we hold him down?'

'No, call a doctor.'

'But look at him!'

And while the people sought ways to be helpful, the spasms continued: mindless, grotesque, irrepressible.

Then it was over. What seemed to have gone on forever had, in fact, lasted scarcely a minute. Stunned and bewildered, Julian's senses staggered their way back to consciousness. What happened?

He was desperate to know. The horror-struck faces suspended above him provided a sobering clue. For the rest, he would have to rely on the competence of his physician, who would later determine he had suffered a brief "grand mal seizure." Diagnosis: Epilepsy—Temporal Lobe.

* * *

My hair won't grow. Not anywhere—on my arms, my legs, or any of the normal places. Worst is my head. I don't think I minded being bald until now. But I saw people stare at me this morning. They've probably been staring all along, and I just haven't noticed. I know now, though. I look funny. I've been standing in front of the mirror for almost an hour trying to decide what to do. It is now 11:52 in the A.M. Monday, September 22nd.

12:30 in the P.M. This is the same day. I just got back. I went out with a scarf on to see if people still stared. I couldn't tell for sure.

When you're looking to see if people are looking at you, they don't look at you the same. I'm going to try again without the scarf.

Same day at 1:15 P.M. I walked all the way to the chapel and back, then right through the cafeteria. Some people stared, some didn't. I suppose the ones who didn't are used to seeing me—though I didn't recognize any of them. I thought of getting a wig, but where? Then I thought I could wear a wimple. Sister Dana would probably lend me one of hers. I've decided to ask her when she comes this afternoon.

Sister Dana's visits to Marcy had come to be a regular part of their days. The feelings of attraction the nun felt for the girl had been forcibly suppressed. "Therapy" was the banner she waved above the growing friendship. And her daily reports on Marcy's progress corroborated this claim. At twenty-six, Sister Dana was considerably older than her charge, and yet the nun's cloistered life made the gap seem far narrower.

'Good afternoon.'

'Good afternoon, Sister.'

'I was told you've already been out today—twice, in fact.'

The girl had been unaccustomed to venturing out alone, and Sister Dana was anxious about the change.

'I'm bald.'

Marcy's bluntness precluded any tiptoeing around the subject.

31

'So you are.'

'All over.'

At this the Sister couldn't help a blush—though she recovered somewhat with her answer.

'And have been since you came.'

'Why?'

This brand of bold questioning was new as well. It took Sister Dana a little by surprise.

'We don't really know. That is, we don't know why your hair hasn't grown back in.'

Immediately she bit her tongue, for her answer implied that Marcy had once had hair, and that the reason she didn't anymore was known. (All information about Marcy's past is to come exclusively from Marcy. Sister Zoë had been quite clear on that point.) She prayed the girl had missed her subtle slip.

'Could I try on your wimple?'

A keener sense of panic seized the nun. Its source was not the possible irreverence involved, but rather Sister Dana's terror at having someone learn her secret, her precious, precious secret. And yet that very prospect sent a thrilling shiver up her spine.

Why shouldn't she share her sacrifice with Marcy?

With a wildly beating heart the young nun weighed the pros and cons.

Then, resolutely, she pulled the wimple from her freshly shaven head.

'You must promise me you will never tell another living soul. Do you promise, Marcy?'

Marcy gaped in disbelief, then solemnly nodded. She couldn't know, of course, that none of the other nuns were similarly shaved, that Sister Dana's exaggerated act had been a private penance. But intuition told her that the symbol was of great importance.

The young nun, cheeks still flushed from boldness, led her confidant to the mirror where she reverently placed her wimple on Marcy's head.

'This, too, must be our secret. Promise?'

'But why?'

'It is forbidden.'

They looked at their reflections, a conspiratorial kinship there aglow.

'You'd make a very pretty nun.'

'You think so? Really?'

'Yes. You're lovely.'

On impulse Sister Dana pressed a kiss to Marcy's cheek. The girl's brow darkened. The nun drew back, horribly regretting her indiscretion. But the shadow passed.

'Why is it forbidden?'

'Because a Sister's raiment can only be conferred by God.'

'You mean God gave this to you?'

'In a way.'

Marcy lifted off the wimple deferentially.

'Have I sinned then?'

'Only a little. But don't worry. I'll say ten Our Fathers on your behalf and the sacrilege will be forgiven.'

Amused by Marcy's innocent distress, Sister Dana failed to note the seriousness with which these last few words were taken.

* * *

On Sunday, Mass was said at dawn. The nuns wore white. Marcy thought them beautiful as she watched their silent exodus from Quarters to the chapel doors. So clean, so pure, so virginal, they floated over the grounds like apparitions. And oh, how much she longed to join them—or rejoin them, for since Sister Dana's revelation, a theory had begun to form in Marcy's mind.

In the past few days her questions about her identity had multiplied. And though this new self-interest was thwarted by a memory gone blank, she still had current events to feed her clues.

Her theory was that her name had once been Sister Marcy. Had not she felt a holy presence while trying on the wimple? And was she not told that her doing so had constituted sacrilege?

Why sacrilege? Unless she was no longer worthy. Unless she had somehow fallen out of favor in the eyes of the Lord. Why else would the chapel be declared off limits to her and her alone?

Could her sin be so unspeakable that it excluded her from the House of God? If so, she feared her loss of hair must be a punishment from Him—never to grow back until she repented. Yet how could she ever make amends when nobody would tell her what she had done? For no matter whom she asked, her questions about her past were all evaded.

The evidence was mounting though, each sign an allegation. She was guilty of something, that much was certain; she simply did not know of what—not yet.

Dejectedly she closed the curtains. The chapel bell tolled. She retreated to her bed, crept in, curled up underneath the blankets, and said a silent prayer for her redemption.

* * *

LAST WILL AND TESTAMENT

On this Friday, the 22nd day of August, I, Julian Papp, being of "reasonably" sound mind and body (for though I'm perfectly aware of what I'm doing, I'd hardly consider myself "in the pink"), make the following provisions for the distribution of my earthy goods (and ashes).

To my Mother Dear,

whose lifelong devotion merits more from her only son than the cruel shock of finding his remains, I leave everything not otherwise bequeathed, but especially I will her my hand-carved chess set given to me by the first Grandmaster who bowed to superior play (i.e. mine). Being my most prized possession, perhaps this gesture will dispel any doubts she may have about my feelings for her. My last act is one she is/was powerless to prevent, even had I made my intentions known. From my point of view, her motherhood was flawless, and thus guiltless.

To my father,

about whose verity my mother thought me unaware, I return my first chess set (sans two lost pawns), which arrived mysteriously by mail on my sixth birthday. Being the only gift I ever received from him before or since (excluding my initial genes—which, alas, have proven suspect) I think it only fitting he should have it.

To Polly Elton,

I leave her last letter, which I framed and hung on the wall above my bed—complete with effusive affirmations of her everlasting love (dated three and a half days before she left me). I trust this "document of female constancy" will find her fat and happy and blithely breeding in Dubuque (or wherever).

To Miriam Jeffries,

who nobly suppressed her secret loathing for my body to soothe its "beautiful soul," I leave a lock of my hair.

Last and intentionally least,

To Mercedes Ballantine,

I bequeath my dark glasses, which, I may rest assured, will be mounted in her trophy room alongside the other ill-gotten mementos of sundry and gullible freaks—for whom she made her shapely legs the unabashed avenues unto ecstasy (once per customer). A pox on her predatory pubes.

Conscience nearly cleared, spleen vented, these closing words will ratify my choice to self-destruct:

Having had the misfortune of being born without pigmentation in my skin, and therefore resembling a kind of whey-faced colorless slug, I have long fought the *stares of an ignorant world whose tolerance for difference is zilch. However, this ongoing struggle—a considerable scourge in my earlier years—has not been without compensation (thus ought to be discounted as my sole justification for suicide). Being conspicuous in the eyes of my peers, I came to discover I had none (peers, that is)— a sort of compensatory snobbery bred of the wasted years spent envying the normal. Freed then from a misguided urge to be considered "of the people" I deliberately set out to emphasize my uniqueness. The makeup my mother well-meaningly bought to enliven my ghastly complexion I discarded. In its place I purchased some talcum powder and a pair of white pajamas. Eventually, my entire wardrobe followed suit.*

It wasn't enough, though, to look different. I had to be different. And chess, glorious chess was my salvation. (As further evidence of my soundness of mind, let it be noted that I am aware of the vain indulgence in this autobiographical outburst and will shortly curtail it.) With a little study and a lot of practice, I discovered that I was not only good but exceptional at the game; I dare say I was unbeatable. Was.

But now I get fits. Not just while playing chess. I get them doing almost everything, but during chess in particular. I cannot tolerate this. My doctor assures

*me that once he has found the appropriate dosage of
anticonvulsants I'll be able to resume competition and
"a normal life". But what no one understands is that I
no longer see the board the way I used to. Before my first
seizure, winning lines were as clear to me as night and
day. I hardly had to concentrate. Now I play as in an
obfuscating fog.*

*It is for this reason that I have decided to terminate
my life. To anyone not me—i.e., everybody else—this
will seem irrational; but from the only relevant vantage
point—my own—it makes perfect sense.*

*May my corpse be burned and set out with the
morning trash.*

Signed,
Julian Papp

***

'But why can't she attend? Most all of the other patients
do.'

'We've been through this before. The other patients
don't have Marcy's problems.'

'But she wants to come. She wants to be a nun.'

'Of course she does. We represent the only life she knows. But don't you think it a bit unfair to indoctrinate the girl before she's had the chance to learn who she is?'

'You talk as if you think our faith will hurt her.'

The old nun sighed. She knew full well what stood behind these fervent protestations. For though Sister Dana's reports maintained a clinical veneer, there were hints a deeper feeling was involved. And Sister Zoë had watched it happen, trusting it would not get out of hand, and at the same time hoping Marcy might respond to the loving care. But could the young nun's faith be counted on to keep her feelings within the limits of propriety? If not, the risk to each was much too great.

'On the contrary, Sister. Our faith can be quite beneficial, but only when those who would embrace it do so of their own free will.'

Sister Dana searched her wits. She and Sister Zoë had argued many times. Outcomes were decided by the sounder reason, not by rank—although to date the younger nun had seldom won.

'Isn't our way the way, Sister Zoë?'

'That is our Church's teaching.'

'Then isn't it our duty to encourage Marcy—for the sake of her immortal soul?'

'The issue still is one of choice. I'm sure, having been among us, Marcy will come to understand that our Savior welcomes any and all who seek Him. But we must lead her to herself if later we are to help her find our Lord.'

'Well I don't see how Marcy's attending services takes away her choice. Doesn't it do just the opposite?'

The point was well taken. Sister Zoë regretted having withheld her real reason for the prohibition. Better to concede the fault, than to air unorthodox views—especially in front of the impressionable Sister Dana.

'It is not the service; it's the chapel.'

Sister Dana failed to follow.

'You're familiar with Marcy's medical file. Consider it for a moment. Now think: what might be upsetting to such a patient about our chapel.'

'I couldn't say. I mean, I'm not sure what you're getting at. Unless…'

The apprehension in Sister Zoë suddenly took shape for Sister Dana. The chapel's crucifix! It was, undeniably, graphic; many felt gruesome. And no less so were the Stations of the Cross. There had been a painful controversy when the works were first installed, Sister Zoë among others vehemently objecting. But the sanitarium's Board of Directors unanimously overruled. The artist had been especially commissioned. Endowment funds had been used. And it was deemed too grave a slight to vote for posthumous rejection, since, within a week of completing the works, the artist had died. Thereafter, the nuns did their level best to counteract the morbid atmosphere—keeping fresh-cut flowers in all the chapel's nooks and crannies—but, even so, it took a while before the faithful could adjust. Those uninitiated often found the chapel shocking.

'I'm sorry for doubting your judgment, Sister.'

'It is I who must apologize to you, Sister Dana. Had I been open with you, this matter might have been easily resolved.'

'I understand, though, Sister.'

'You do, yes. I'm glad. But what about Marcy?'

'Oh.'

'You told her you were coming to see me?'

'Yes.'

'So she'll be disappointed if I don't change my decision. How disappointed?'

'Very, Sister.'

'I should have foreseen this. When are you going to see her?'

'As soon as I leave here.'

'Send her to me immediately.'

'Yes, Sister. I'm sorry, Sister.'

The older nun held up her hand.

'No need, no need. The fault is entirely mine.'

Sister Dana rose to go. The other nun stopped her.

'By the way, you argued very well.'

She flushed with pride.

'Thank you, Sister Zoë.'

When she had gone the nun retreated to her chair.

She was pensive. The rebuttal she had withheld came into mind. (Isn't our way the way?) She shook her head. Religion was too dear a friend to politics. And doctrine much too often corroborated power. Insisting there was one and only one way to salvation was a prime example. Nonsense. If that were true, there would be no use for fertile imaginations. And would not faith be dull indeed if every searching soul trod the selfsame path. Sister Zoë believed there were as many avenues to God as there were men—and women; finding each his or her own was life's adventure.

Though how she had tailored this and other controversial views to fit her habit was at times as much a mystery to herself as to her peers. She dared question, sometimes even challenge, what most believed to be the very tenets of Catholicism. But it was her critics who suffered, not her faith—a faith grown strong from the exercise her reason gave it.

She heard a knock.

Marcy must have run. She panted hello and took the seat that Sister Zoë offered. Her hasty arrival found the nun's plan yet unformulated.

'I didn't expect you so soon. Are you all right?'

Marcy caught her breath.

'Sister Dana said, "immediately".'

'And here you are.'

'Am I too early?'

'I don't think one can be too early for immediately. No, you're right on time. Thank you for coming.'

She paused to evaluate once again this touchy situation. The girl was nervous, anxious, no doubt hopefully expectant, and hung upon the imminent decision... which the nun now made.

'I would like to invite you formally to attend our Sunday service.'

Marcy was overjoyed.

'Oh, Sister!'

'You haven't seen our chapel, have you?'

'Only from the outside.'

'Perhaps you'll let me show it to you.'

'Now, you mean? Right now?'

'Immediately.'

Marcy sprang to her feet and was at the door before her escort left her chair. She had to wait, however, as the old nun took her time. Together then, they set out toward the chapel.

* * *

Thursday, October 2nd, at 9:09 in the A.M. I've been inside the chapel! Sister Zoë gave me a special tour. It's awful! Not the chapel. What they did to Jesus. There were pictures all along the walls showing it. We went by them one by one with Sister telling the story. His eyes were the saddest eyes I've ever seen. They made me cry and Sister was going to take me away but I said no. We kept walking and Sister kept talking but I didn't have to listen. I knew the second I saw his face how the story ended. Then we were standing under him. I almost couldn't look, but I did. I had to.

He was dying. Sister tried to explain why and what it all meant. I didn't hear though. I heard something else, like pounding. I think it was his heart. I heard it beating.

Then another sound came. It got louder and louder until I couldn't hear the heartbeat anymore. It was the insect sound, shrill and terrible, and then I screamed.

I guess Sister didn't know what to do because she just let me, until I stopped. Then he was dead. He still had his eyes open and the blood trickling down all over and his hands and feet all crippled from the pain, but he didn't feel it anymore.

And I was glad. They'd hurt him so bad, I was glad it was over. I stopped crying then.

Sister led me away. She was saying how he'd gone to be with his father and wasn't really dead and in three days was alive again, but I think she was just trying to make me feel better. I was all right though. Him up there on the cross, and the pictures, didn't bother me anymore.

We walked back here and Sister made me lie down to rest. I didn't think I was tired but I was wrong, I guess, because I slept until this morning. I think I dreamed.

As soon as I woke up I was supposed to go see Sister. But I remembered everything and wanted to write it down first. I forgot the dream.

During the incident in the chapel, Sister Zoë again confronted what she believed to be the specter of Marcy's past. For though the girl's response could not be attributed unequivocally to her memory of the rape, it was a logical (and an intuitive) assumption. The fact that Marcy appeared unacquainted with the crucifixion and the story of Christ suggested that religion had something to do with her identity. But was it identity-related prior to Marcy's coming, or had it been a recent adjustment corresponding to the young girl's interest in the Sisterhood? The puzzle was complex. Waiting now for Marcy to arrive, the nun suspected it would grow no simpler.

Where was the girl? As usual Sister Zoë, up at 6:00, had showered, dressed, and prayed, then gone outdoors to take her morning constitutional. By 8:00 she had eaten breakfast. At 8:15 she had presided over the meeting called to inform her staff about a new admission: reviewing the patient's background, assessing his present needs, selecting the ward to which he would be assigned. At 9:00 she had checked the note left pinned to her door in case Marcy had come during her absence—and found she had not. At 9:45 she had welcomed the new patient. At 10:15 she had returned to read and answer the daily mail. And here it was 11:30 and there was still no sign of Marcy.

I saw him! I was on my way to see Sister when I saw this car pull up and he got out. I recognized him instantly. He was exactly like the carving that the Miniature Man had made. And white! He was all white, too. Not just his clothes. Everything! His hair, his skin. I couldn't believe it. I hid. I don't know why. I didn't want him to see me. But he did anyway. Or at least I think he did because he turned and looked right at the tree where I was hiding. He had on dark glasses so I couldn't see his eyes. I ducked out of sight. Then I ran. I don't know if he was still watching. I didn't turn. I ran straight back here.

I wish I'd told Sister about the carving before. She probably won't believe me if I tell her now. I wish he hadn't seen me. I wish I knew the reason why...

There was a knock on the door. Marcy jumped.

'Marcy… Marcy?'

The door slowly opened.

'Marcy?'

Marcy saw feet—they were Sister Dana's. She was so relieved she almost came out from her hiding place. Embarrassment prevented her. How could she explain why she was acting like a little child? She waited, a hot blush throbbing in her ears. It seemed to take forever for the door to close.

When it did she crawled back out from under her

bed. Her journal still lay open on the desk, its last line waiting—I wish I knew the reason why... She finished it... he's come.

* * *

'According to this report, Mr. Papp, you either refuse to take your medication or you gulp it all at once. Have you never heard the adage, "everything in moderation, nothing in excess"?'

'You're a great one to talk. When was the last time you had sex, Ms. Zoë?'

'Longer ago than you could—or I'd care to—remember. And it is *Sister* Zoë. Now, your doctor has prescribed Tegretol and Mysoline. To be taken daily. Have you done so today?'

'I have not.'

'You forgot, then? Or did Sister Clara neglect to take it to you this morning?'

'Oh, it was there all right, on a tray no less—impotence on a silver platter.'

'Are you referring to the drugs' ineffectiveness?'

'Just the contrary. I haven't had an erection in weeks.'

'Listen, Julian. May I call you Julian?'

He let a stony silence answer.

'Mr. Papp, then. Things will be a lot more pleasant if we can work together. You were allowed to leave the hospital, remember, because you made an agreement to cooperate.'

'I'd have agreed to Leavenworth to get out of that sensory-deprivation tank.'

'So your promise was a false one?'

'It wasn't a promise; it was a confession. I couldn't stand it there anymore so I signed. They beat it out of me, Father.'

'*Sister*.'

'Tongue depressors under my fingernails, disinfectants in my food, dope injections and ice water enemas—it was hell, absolute hell.'

'And were these "cruel and unusual punishments" necessary to prevent you from attempting suicide again?'

'If not necessary, at least successful, for here I am.'

'Willing or unwilling to cooperate?'

'I promise never to *attempt* the terminal deed again.'

'Mr. Papp, we haven't the staff to watch you day and night. If you're really determined to kill yourself, you'll find it easy to do so here. Therefore, it might be better…'

'You're not thinking of sending me back? Mother of Mercy, not that! I'd sooner survive.'

'How is it, Mr. Papp, that someone with such a hearty sense of humor can be so fatalistic?'

'Let me consider… "Life is the one joke from which we all die laughing"… or… You see? They've so befuddled my brain with their pharmacological charity I can hardly manage to answer clichés in kind. What's to become of me?'

'Let's see if we can work that out. Will you agree to come and talk to me if ever you feel deeply depressed?'

'A contract?'

'I beg your pardon?'

'Suicide Prevention Center jargon: placing an intermediary between the client and his threatened act. I'm surprised you're unfamiliar with…'

'I know the term. Well?'

'Will you call off your spies?'

'Spies?'

'Ms. Clara and that bald girl.'

'Marcy? Where did you meet Marcy?'

'We haven't met. She runs away every time I catch sight of her. First time was the day I got here. She was watching from behind a tree.'

'How odd… Marcy is not a staff member; she's a patient. As for Sister Clara, she has been assigned to help you get acquainted with the lifestyle here. She will do anything she can to make your stay with us more comfortable.'

'Thanks, but no thanks. She's not my type. Now, if the bald kid were a few years older…'

'Mr. Papp, I find your consistent use of sexual innuendo

of interest only professionally; it is personally quite obnoxious. If it is something you would like to discuss, fine. I suspect, however, it is more a case of bad manners. But what is merely a minor irritation to me could be quite damaging to a patient, and I suggest, if you have any desire to stay on here, you demonstrate a bit more respect for others—as well as for yourself.'

'You have a peculiar bedside manner yourself, Ms. Zoë. What if I were the sensitive type and your chewing me out sent me plummeting into the "slough of despond"? My death would be on your head, wouldn't it?'

'Firstly, I don't think you're that delicate psychologically. Secondly, your death as well as your life is in God's hands, not in yours or mine.'

'You must be kidding. I can see the costume and all— the beads, the wimple, the crucifix—but surely you've come to realize psychiatry and Catholicism are hopelessly incompatible. Or is that diploma on your wall back there in "Faith Healing"?'

'I take it, then, that you are not religious?'

'If there's a God, I'm a monkey's uncle. Whereas if there isn't, the monkey's *my* uncle—and I believe Mr. Darwin proved that rather convincingly.'

'You're very clever, Mr. Papp. But are you bright enough to have wondered, to have asked the question why, to have plumbed your imagination for a primary cause?'

'The "Big Bang" will do.'

'Yes, but who set the charge?'

'Personally, I'd vote for the abominable snowman. But others—with equally inane justification—have latched onto a more anthropomorphic character—invariably old, wise, male, and Caucasian.'

'And with so little faith you still can live?'

'Zugzwang! Though you'll be hard-pressed to attribute my existential apathy to atheism.'

'Why do you want to end your life?'

'I doubt you'd understand.'

'Try me.'

'All right. Imagine that through constant prayer and meditation you were able to achieve a certain rapport with your God. It was like an open channel through which some "quintessential meaning" flowed. Then one fine day an illness struck you down, and when you recovered, you realized the channel had been closed. What would be the point of going on?'

'Could you use your own case as an example instead of analogizing mine?'

'Chess, goddamn it! I can't play anymore.'

'Since your overdose?'

'No, since my first seizure.'

'Have you tried?'

'I played my computer.'

'And?'

'It beat me. It never beats me. Even on its slowest speed.'

'You had been through quite an ordeal, though, hadn't you?'

'When you look the way I do, ordeals are quotidian. No, you don't understand. I used to see the right moves. I'd go to a special place in my mind, completely relax, and when I'd come back the moves were obvious.'

'What kind of place?'

'I can't describe it. I tried to tell my doctor, but as soon as he could slap on the medical term—"aura" he called it—he stopped listening.'

'I'll listen.'

'What's the use? It's gone.'

'Did your doctor explain how auras generally work?'

'That they're warning signs a seizure's about to happen—or is in fact happening? Yes.'

'But you used to get the auras without suffering the convulsions.'

'Yeah, I guess so—if aura is the right name for what I experienced.'

'Did he also tell you that it's not unusual for epileptics to forget the aura after a seizure, especially after a grand mal seizure?'

'Implying that I still go to my meadow but just can't remember? What's the difference? Either way it's lost.'

'So it's a meadow you used to visit?'

'What?'

'You said, "my meadow". Is it a place you recall from real life or is it imaginary?'

'This interview is over.'

Julian rose, spun around, and defiantly left the room.

* * *

'… relaxed… almost sleeping… relaxed… and sound… sound… asleep… Can you hear me, Marcy?'

'Yes.'

'Do you know where you are?'

'Elevator.'

'That's right. You are back in your own private elevator ready for bed. In just a moment the doors are going to open and you will step out into your room. The bed will be waiting, all turned down, with freshly laundered sheets. Are you ready?'

'Yes.'

'The doors are opening. You're stepping out.'

The room was just as she had left it, except her bed was made, its covers folded back like a table napkin. The sheets looked so inviting she could barely wait to nestle in between them. A pleasant breeze lilted in through the open window, dancing with the curtains.

'You're walking to your bed. Are you there?'

'Yes.'

'In you go. And when I count three, you'll be fast asleep. Your sleep will last for five full minutes, during which time you will dream. It will be a dream about your earlier life, before you came to St. Francis. Your family will be there and you may talk to them. When the dream has ended, you will open your eyes. You'll be sitting in my office. You will feel fresh and rested and wide awake. Do you understand?'

'Yes.'

'One… Two… Three.'

The Miniature Man sat in a rocking chair, his features lit diffusively by the crackling embers in a makeshift stove and by the massive drip candle flickering light and shadow over his ever-whittling hands. Beyond these humble aureoles the wondrous paraphernalia in the room was lost to darkness. Marcy, therefore, picked her way with caution. She felt her presence had been noted, even though the eccentric little man had not looked up. There was an empty chair beside him, plainly set for her to sit in—which she did.

There seemed no hurry. The man rocked slowly, very much at ease. Marcy found the rocking's gentle cadence soothing. She waited calmly for the conversation (if there was indeed to be one) to begin.

Been a while, young Miss.

His voice blended so well with the rocker's steady creaking it was barely audible. Remembering then the peculiar requisite for making cordial speech, Marcy answered silently.

I've tried to visit but I can never seem to find you on my own.

You'll find me whenever it's necessary.

Is that true?

The old man glanced at her out of the corner of his monocled eye. He nodded with his brows.

How long can you stay?

Five minutes.

His rocking halted.

Five minutes! That's criminal, ridiculous, absolutely aggravating! It's that worry-wrinkled nun again, isn't it? She brought you.

Yes.

His rocking resumed at an accelerated clip.

Stingy, grasping, over-protective, religious fana...

He broke off the tirade, slowed his chair.

Well, nothing to be done. Might as well get on with it.

On with what?

Give you what you've come for.

But I haven't come for any...

Of course you have. Still don't know yourself very well, do you?

He put aside the piece of wood on which he was working and began searching his pockets.

It's here somewhere... Stuck it in just... Ah ha, found it.

His hand came from inside his flannel vest in a tight-closed fist, knobby knuckles bulging, veins stretched smooth. The image of the old man's first gift flashed through Marcy's mind. How had he known about the man in white? More pressing, though, was her discovering what the outstretched hand concealed. Its burnished palm turned upward, fingers gracefully uncurling, until another perfect carving was revealed.

57

Marcy recognized the form. There, in every minuscule detail, was Sister Dana.

As she reached for it, however, he closed his hand.

A poisoned pawn.

What's that?

Ask the paleface King.

Who?

The new patient.

He chuckled. Marcy's look was still perplexed.

That anemic-looking fellow you've been hiding from for the last two weeks—without, I might add, the least regard for my advice! Of course you'll do what you will do. But he's the one to ask about the poisoned pawn.

But I'm scared of him. I see him walking around the grounds late at night like a ghost. He looks blind. I know he sees, though. He sees me. He always does. No matter how I try to look without him noticing, he turns and stares right at me. It's spooky, the way he drifts around, never making a sound, always by himself—white and thin and moonlit and always knowing where I'm hiding; knowing though I

haven't even dared to peek, changing his direction, coming toward me, closer, closer!

Wide awake, Marcy sat in Sister Zoë's office. Her momentary panic vanished. But all the images remained. She braced herself for Sister's questions. What to tell, what to keep unanswered?

'Did you see something, Marcy, that frightened you?'

Once again the patient had defied suggestions, awakening on her own volition.

'Yes, Sister. Sort of, I mean. I saw that boy in white.'

Did she mean Julian? The nun was mystified. And intrigued.

'Can you describe him?'

'You know. The one who always wears those spooky sunglasses.'

So she had seen him. Not surprising; Julian was very hard to miss. But his appearing in the girl's subconscious was most perplexing.

'Have you two met?'

Now was her chance to tell Sister about the carving and the Miniature Man knowing things, and about the carving of Sister Dana, too, and to ask about the poisoned pawn. But she was not supposed to ask Sister that. And besides she did not feel like telling. She was tired.

'I'm tired. May I go back to my room now?'

Sister Zoë thought it best not to press too hard. Further questions, for the moment, would have to wait.

The knocks on Marcy's door were almost soundless—three soft raps. It was a signal that had come to be routine. Tonight, however, the young girl failed to answer. Instead, she watched… as a rectangle of hall light spread its shape across the floor then quickly shrank as Sister Dana deftly entered. Marcy closed her eyes. The nun approached, drew up a chair beside the bed, sat down, got settled—listening all the while to Marcy's breathing… waiting… listening.

At last she whispered.

'Are you awake?'

The girl lay still, did not respond. Would Sister Dana do the usual: light the lamp, modestly clear her throat, and read a passage or two from the gospels, read softly until her patient fell asleep? Like many of the things they had come to share, this, too, was a secret—although Marcy, in light of the Miniature Man's caution, was beginning to wonder why. She could not imagine how Sister Dana could pose a threat of any kind. Perhaps this vigilance would produce an indication.

The silence in the room began to weigh heavily. What was Sister doing? Marcy longed to peek but was afraid the nun would see. She heard a subtle rustling sound, the sound of cloth. She sensed it stir. Feigning as naturally as she could a sleepy head-toss, she freed her ears. The rustling stopped.

A minute passed. Then gradually she became aware of Sister Dana's breathing. At first it mirrored her own. But soon it quickened… grew more pronounced… breathier… shivery… full of little hitches… faster, faster, faster, until, with a last inhaling gasp, it halted! Marcy's heart throbbed sixteen beats before she heard the breath escape with a long alleviating sigh.

A kiss was tendered lovingly on Marcy's motionless lips. The rectangle of light swept to and fro. Darkness, with confusion, settled in.

It's Saturday, October 17th at 12:03 in the A.M. I can't sleep. I have too much on my mind. Tonight Sister Dana came into my room to read to me like usual only I pretended I was already asleep. I did that because the Miniature Man told me she was a poisoned pawn. Now, I didn't know just what that was, or is, but it didn't sound good. And I definitely got the idea to watch out. So I figured if Sister Dana thought I was sleeping she might do something she wouldn't do normally. She did! I don't want to write down what, because I can't be sure. I had to keep my eyes closed. But after, she kissed me on the mouth and went away.

What's kept me awake is the feeling I got when she was doing what she was doing. It was sickening. I didn't know how, though. Not until she'd gone and I started to think. Then it got bad. The insects came.

When that happens I have to scream to stop the horrible noise. I must have buried my face in the pillow because nobody came. I don't want that ever to happen again. But I don't know what to do. I can't tell Sister Zoë because I promised not to. And the Miniature Man is no help either. He doesn't come whenever I want. And anyway, he says I have to ask the new patient.

I'm scared of him. He's the man in ivory and also this oddball patient who wears sunglasses at night. I don't understand what he has to do with anything, but more and more I'm thinking I'm going to have to ask him some things. Like what he's doing here. And if he knows the Miniature Man. And what a poisoned pawn is.

* * *

The dim horizon, as yet an indistinctive silhouette, forewarned the dawn. Julian stared, depressed by its dumb inevitability. He had haunted each of the sanitarium's surrounding hills in turn, on night-walks—lonely, restive, autumn-chilled, pointless. The chess games, playing in random moves inside his weary head, went unattended. They had disarranged through want of concentration, and now were simply scribbled lines, a dense cross-hatching, occasionally countermanding thought—though unintelligibly. The agreement he had struck with Sister

Zoë looked forever hopeless. Alive for what? The game was over. What use was living? He had resigned; why insist the mating moves be played? It was sadistic; it mocked; it demeaned; it was equivalent to castration with a blunt-edged blade.

With grim dejection he surveyed the scene below— a cluster of stuccoed buildings tucked away in the mountainous wilds of northern Arizona, St. Francis of the Mogollon Rim. It seemed an unlikely place for a mental institution, though it was hardly that in any formal sense. How could it be, run as it was by this offshoot of an offshoot of Franciscan nuns, half of whom were highly trained psychologists, the others merely altruistic novices? And what an eclectic clientele: tubercular patients, Alzheimer's cases, alcoholics, people dying of AIDS, along with lunatics of various infirmity, and a few State referrals (when the State was confronted with a problem for which it had no category).

Julian's mother had heard of St. Francis while crusading to "save her boy"—said effort, for her, automatically leading to their neighborhood priest. He had recommended the sanitarium in glowing, hallowed terms, "a Godly island of Christian Grace where rest and faith and good clean air can heal the ravaged soul". Bolstered by so holy an endorsement, his mother had packed his bags, gotten him discharged from the hospital, and, after a long and tedious journey, delivered him into the merciful hands of God—i.e., Sister Zoë, for at St. Francis it was she who ruled supreme.

The eastern sky grew brighter, its early rays intruding. He cursed it for its uninvited warmth. He walked on sullenly, allowing gravity to guide him through the evaporated night, his steady cadence kindling an argument with time.

How he had watched them—the second, the minute, the hour, those increments of doom, ticking away on the clock as though their march connoted truth—which, of course, it did in real terms, the terms of mutual agreement, the terms of common consent. What other terms were there? His "visions"—where time had no hold, where moments were indistinguishable from days? Those visions were "auras", he had been informed. The term was one on which everyone had agreed. And therefore what he had mistaken for a realm beyond time's tyranny was no more than a symptom of disease. And how could one give credence to a perception based on that?

Yet without respite from linear time, delusional or otherwise, how was one expected to prevail?

Time was pernicious; he knew its force. It paralyzed the will. It made winning moves impossible to find. And worst of all it nullified the poetry, inundating the mind with one unalterable rhythm: tick tock, tick tock, white black, black white, white to move, punch the clock, stop the time, black to move, punch the clock, stop the time, start the time, stop the time, start the time, *MATE*!

He stopped abruptly, images of clock hands and chessmen reeling through his head. A nauseating vertigo assaulted his perceptions, throwing him off balance, triggering the dreaded cry that signified the onset of a fit.

Upon regaining consciousness, Julian lay looking upward into a curious pair of prepossessing eyes.

'Are you okay?'

They shone with a mixture of amazement and compassion.

'I saw you fall. Did you get hurt?'

And were set off rather quaintly by a runny nose.

His senses rallied. Light! Up thrust Julian's hand to claim his property—his dark glasses—snatching them away and hurriedly fixing them in place.

'I-I found them next to you. They must have come off when you fell. I saw you fall.'

'You said that.'

He sat up. His clothes were sopping but he was otherwise unscathed.

'You were kind of squirming around like you were in a lot of pain.'

He marshaled his wits. Having donned his disguise again, he felt less vulnerable—and besides, she was just a kid.

'No, no pain. Never any pain. Just a little something I

do to entertain the wildlife.'

He stood up. Marcy backed away a step.

'Don't worry; it's not contagious.'

She stared at him with redoubled fascination—which he bore impatiently.

'You'll drool keeping up that gape.'

'Sorry. It's just that you look exactly like him.'

'I resemble someone you know? Marcy, you must have a very strange pack of friends.'

She started again.

'How do you know my name? Did the Miniature Man tell you?'

'The who? Hey, kid, you don't make much sense. I know you're a patient. But are you one of the loony ones?'

'No! No. And I'm not a kid, either. I'm probably as old as you.'

'I doubt that. Don't let my complexion fool you. Beneath this baby-powder veneer, I'm an aged man of twenty. You can't be over twelve.'

'Oh, no; I'm at least thirteen and I might be as old as fifteen, sixteen even.'

'Don't you know?'

'None of your business.'

Julian's superior attitude had begun to annoy her. She, after all, had rushed to help him, and by way of thanks, he seemed to want to make fun of her.

'What's under the cap?'

She reached up to the knit hat she wore, making sure it was still secure.

'My head, what else?'

'I'll wager very little.'

He smiled. She disliked the smile; it was too much like a smirk. She disliked its implications, too. Defiantly, she snatched off her hat.

'There! Anything more you'd like to say? People who make fun of other people are just covering up for what they don't like in themselves.'

'Sounds like a Zoëian platitude.'

'"Zoëian"? Sister Zoë, you mean? She didn't tell me that. I'm not stupid, you know. I think for myself.'

Her pluck amused him. It irritated him some, too. He had tried to even the score—his seeing her bald head for her seeing his pink eyes. It was a reflex of petty meanness of which he was a little ashamed—considering the difference in their ages. He decided to mollify her.

'Your eyes have already told me you're not stupid.'

She picked through his words to see if there were any traces of nastiness, then blushed—on realizing he had just paid her a compliment.

'I didn't mean to look at yours. I wouldn't have if I'd known.'

'Known what?'

She struggled.

'That it made you mad.'

'"Mad"?'

'Embarrassed, I mean.'

'"Embarrassed"?'

'Self-…' She stopped. 'It doesn't matter what word I use, does it?'

No dresser's dummy here. He was impressed. A little competition might prove amusing. He retreated—to draw her back in.

'You're right. It makes me self-conscious. I'm fully aware I look like an oversized rabbit.'

'I didn't think that at all! You shouldn't make jokes about yourself like that.'

The play for sympathy worked. He had exposed a weakness.

'Would lab rat be more apropos?'

'Now you're just feeling sorry for yourself.'

Or had he? She had countered that well. He realigned his defenses, changing the point of attack.

'So, what are you in for? Burglary? Murder? Rape?'

A strangling lump arose in Marcy's throat. Her limbs went numb. She fought for control. But the insect sounds were already buzzing cruelly in her ears. She used the only means she knew to make them stop.

Her shriek took Julian totally by surprise. He staggered backward. Yet through his shock he saw the girl's hysteria retract, collapsing in on itself as if greedily reabsorbed.

And before he was even aware that the scream had carried to the grounds below, a triumvirate of attendants had arrived.

With neither question nor reprimand, two nuns bracketed Marcy, who let herself be spirited away. A third nun stayed to determine the cause of Julian's disheveled condition. He looked at her contemptuously, then marched off toward his quarters unescorted.

* * *

'Was there anything different you noticed about the seizure?'

'No.'

'Can you reconstruct your thoughts and actions just prior?'

'No.'

'Have you been taking your medication?'

'No.'

Sister Zoë was exasperated.

'Mr. Papp, you promised that…'

'I wouldn't kill myself. I didn't promise I'd swallow those horse pills.'

'What do you expect, then?'

'I can only hope.'

'The seizures won't kill you.'

'Unless I'm precariously perched when one hits.'

'Is that your plan—passive suicide? If it is, I'll have to insist you be accompanied on all your walks—the after curfew ones, as well.'

'I thought you didn't have the staff for that.'

'Julian… Mr. Papp, I thought we agreed that it was in your best interests to remain here until your convulsions were under control and you felt well enough to return home. Dr. Cahill has changed your prescription to amend the side effect about which you complained, so taking…'

'Which one was that, Ms. Zoë?'

'It was my understanding you were experiencing a lack of sexual potency.'

'Ah, yes. Quite right. Limp as a noodle.'

'Well, that should no longer trouble you.'

'Oh, Ms. Zoë, you can't imagine how reassuring that will be for all my ladies-in-waiting.'

'Spare me your wit.'

'And spoil the child? It's a thought. She's no doubt willing. But is she old enough to know how?'

The nun slapped her hand down on her desk.

'Enough! If it is Marcy to whom you are referring, I will not caution you again. She is in a very delicate psychological state…'

'Unlike mine.'

'… and any further insensitivity you show toward her will not be tolerated! Do I make myself clear?'

'As the chapel bell.'

'Good.'

'What's her problem, anyway?'

'It is our policy not to discuss the…'

'I see. You cultivate sensitivity by keeping people ignorant—a method your church considers tried and true, I believe. But has it occurred to you that if I knew something about the girl, that banshee number she pulled this morning might not be repeated?'

The nun was sorry she had lost her temper. The incident had been reported to her and she had intended to compare versions; Marcy's had not been overly helpful. She was counting on Julian to shed more light. But now he was on the defensive.

For Julian's part, the puzzle of Marcy's bizarre behavior had aroused his curiosity. He remembered precisely what he had said, but had "burglary" or "murder" or "rape" been the catchword?

What did her not knowing her own age imply? Why was she hairless? The more he dwelled on her, the more he was intrigued.

'You say you don't recall what happened just before the seizure. What about afterward?'

He resented her avoiding his question.

'My mind's a blank.'

'Oh, come now, Mr. Papp. You don't really expect me to accept a claim of feeble memory from a chess master.'

He considered a moment. The flattery was a bit transparent, but perhaps he could gain some time, manipulate her into offering an exchange. It was worth a try.

'When I opened my roseate eyes, two hazel mirrors bounced back my reflection. I didn't look well. Of course that's understandable considering I'd just performed my human earthquake routine. Nonetheless, the eyes that stared unblinkingly finally blinked, relieving me of the spectacle of myself—which enabled me to take in my surroundings. Weeds—tall, wet, smelling faintly of sod and cow dung—ensconced my head. My canopy was two parts sky, one part female. The sky was approximating blue. The female hovered between flesh tones and an adolescent crimson; I fear she blushed for me. I sat. The blood deserted my addled brain then casually reentered. Lucidity, alas, bestowed its blessing. Not only had my comely antics soaked and soiled my clothes, they had drawn an audience. Perfect. I rose to take a bow. The girl—my single fan—backed up, overwhelmed no doubt by the proximity of her idol. I thought her failure to applaud a trifle rude, but she managed to stammer a comment or two in praise. Appeased, I engaged her in a "normal" conversation during which: she dared compare me to another, mentioned a miniature man, expressed confusion about her age, exposed her shaven head, lectured me on man's inhumanity to man, and finally ended on a piquant note *screamed* at the top of her lungs. All in all a remarkable performance in its own right, don't you think?'

Sister Zoë had been tempted to interrupt this impudent monologue, but mixed with Julian's elaborate deprecations were valuable bits that did ring true—though not enough to piece together the whole of what had happened.

'Is that all the detail you can muster, Mr. Papp?'

'Detail? Those were merely the skeletal facts. I can be as comprehensive as the tiny mole on Marcy's cheek—the left cheek, I believe—a pinhead mole not raised but flush to her nubile—nay cherubic—skin. There was a second one, too, as I recall, just below the right corner of her mouth, a mouth like a cherry stain—sweet, puffy-lipped, profoundly kissable. The girl is bald, of course, but it's a feature not altogether hideous, for she has a rather shapely skull, good cheekbones, sturdy chin. Her face might even be considered beautiful if it weren't so young. But naïveté drips from Marcy's phiz like snot from a runny nose.'

'Perhaps, Mr. Papp, a compromise might be reached between your describing too…'

'Compromise? I'm amenable to compromise. I'll even offer you a handicap. For every two questions I answer of yours, you answer one of mine.'

'So you don't intend to tell me what happened unless I

betray a patient's confidence? Sorry, Mr. Papp, no deal.'

'Three questions to one?'

'And further, you are to stay as far away from Marcy as possible. Is that understood?'

'You're sounding like the chapel bell again.'

'We will talk again tomorrow morning when you come *at nine* to take your medication.'

'You want to watch? I guess there's a little voyeur in us all, eh, Ms. Zoë?'

'You may go.'

It had been a long time since the personality of a patient had gotten under Sister Zoë's skin. But Julian's definitely had. He had even made her feel an old fool, and she was unsure precisely how he had done it. She had encountered comparable intellects in the past—some rivaling Julian's cynicism, too. What made him such an exacerbating exception?

She watched from her window as his spectral figure crossed the common, heading toward the solace of the evergreens, alone. That aloneness was probably Julian's worst enemy, yet the first interest he had shown in anything outside his brooding solitude—his interest in Marcy—she had summarily forbidden. Had she acted rightly?

She returned to her desk to commit her doubts to paper.

Without a sound, Sister Dana closed her Bible's leather cover. She dimmed the light. The room took on a cozy ambiance, so sweet, so coveted—Marcy close and lovely (enveloped by a patchwork quilt the nun herself had made), fast asleep. At such idyllic times, she yearned to speak, use her prayer voice, bare her soul. She had been so lonely before this precious girl had come! Her covenant with God had failed to bring the ecstasies once envisioned, those of the Saints whose wondrous lives had touched her own, as a child, through stories told to her and read to her over and over by her father. She had betrayed him. Not on the surface (proud father, rejoicing in his daughter's final vows, had actually knelt and kissed her stockinged feet), but rather in her heart-of-hearts, where she harbored certain doubts, and where she feared she would forever prove unworthy. And now she had truly fallen, lavishing the love pledged to God onto someone else, plotting in the dark, nourishing thoughts and feelings she knew to be sinful. She removed her wimple. The badge of her devotion mirrored the pate of her beloved—shaved for Marcy, sacrificed for Marcy; not, as she had tried and tried to convince herself, for Him. And this had been a terrible admission. It made her daily ritual with the razor almost vile, a shameless demonstration of depravity. Yet she dared to persist, seduced by the thrill of union she felt with her ward.

'Nothing, Marcy, nothing will compel me to forsake thee.'

Tenderly she tucked the quilt around the girlish body.

'How radiant you are, my sweet. The hair that strangely will not grow could scarcely make your countenance more disarming.'

She lightly fondled a fold in the pillow, then thought to slip her fingers underneath her habit. But this she knew was apostasy, and she resisted—though the tides of love that ebbed and flowed through every passage of her being had persuaded her (at times) to set them free. (And were not certain states, to which this profanation lifted her, higher than any ever known through prayer?)

Marcy stirred. The nun recoiled with guilt. She had sinned again—in thought, if not in deed. The precepts of her faith felt like a noose, a shrinking collar, that kept choking off her happiness, garroting her conscience. With condemnatory fervor she drew her hand up to her breast and forced her fingernails to clutch, sink in, and squeeze.

Marcy's eyelids opened. The nun recovered.

'Still awake? You've had a trying day, my sweet. It's time to sleep, to dream. A dream can take you anywhere, remember. It can wrap you up in loving arms and carry you to Ithaca, or Katmandu, or Rome. Sleep. Close your pretty eyes, my love, and sleep.'

Suspended in the murky void between fact and unreality, Marcy allowed her wits to re-submerge.

* * *

Monday, October 20th, at 9:30 in the A.M. I feel better today. Lots has happened. Last night, when I couldn't sleep, I got dressed and went out. You're not supposed to but I've seen Julian do it—I asked, and that's his name—so why shouldn't I? I saw him. He was a long way off. This time, though, he didn't turn to stare at me. Instead, he made this pitiful sound and fell down on the ground. I ran to help him. When I got there he was shaking all over. I was afraid to touch him. Then it stopped and he opened his eyes. They're pink! With red pupils! The sun had just come up so I was sure. He didn't like me looking at them. He was nasty.

Julian isn't a very nice person, I found out. But I think it's because he doesn't like himself. He makes cruel jokes at his own expense. They're funny, but they don't make you want to laugh. Anyway, we talked a little, and I was going to maybe ask the questions I had planned, when he said something really awful. It must have been, because the insects came. But I don't remember what. All I know is that I screamed, and some nuns came and took me to Sister Zoë. She tried to find out what happened and didn't like that I couldn't tell her. Still, she was patient with me. She asked me to keep away from Julian from now on. She wanted me to promise, but I got out of it without having to. Then she sent for Sister Dana, who took me back to my room and stayed with me the rest of the day.

It's odd, but since Julian's come, I haven't thought much about my past. Except I know I'm not a nun. That was just a dumb idea I had. I don't think that I want to be one, either. There's something unnatural about it.

***

The new routine required Julian to take his medication in Sister Zoë's presence. This brought him to her office every day at nine o'clock. Usually the nun was waiting, tablets in hand. He would saunter in, thrust a few irreverent jabs at psychiatry or religion, spurn the proffered water, raise an empty glass, and, proposing some scatological toast, gulp the pills down dry. Today, however, though the pills, the glass, and the water jug were there, Sister Zoë was not.

Immediately he seized his opportunity—the files! Having had his requests for information categorically denied, his thoughts had turned toward surreptitious means. Short of contriving elaborate plots, there seemed two possibilities: either the records cabinet itself or the desk drawer where its key was kept would be open. Either demanded only the old nun's temporary absence (though the longer the better, for he dared not steal the folder outright).

The files were locked.

The drawer?

Locked, too.

Remembering a trick for opening teachers' desks at school, he pulled out a lower drawer then tried again. Open! And the key was there! Now his enemy was time, the indomitable adversary. In seconds the files were breached, his fingers rifling through the alphabet to "M." No Marcy. Of course. He kicked himself at the oversight. What was the girl's last name? He could hardly expect to have the leisure to canvass case by case. But what else could he do? Time, like damp breath, panted down his neck. He cursed its wretched doggedness. Back or front? A or Z? Z, then. Empty folders. Blank, blank, blank, more blanks, blank, blank, blank, Marcy! Marcy————? No last name? Hastily he pulled her file and read.

At 10:15 Sister Zoë returned to find her office as she had left it, with the exception that the pills set out for Julian were gone. Had he taken them, she wondered? For five straight days he had done so, and had not suffered a single seizure; at least, he had reported none. Perhaps the daily grimaces she was forced to watch (as Julian made taking medicine a kind of martyrdom) were paying off. Once it was demonstrated that, with the drugs, he could maintain control, she hoped his damaged self-esteem would mend; control seemed what he valued most, command of every situation, mastery—oblique and total.

But to have a patient whose status quo depended on the reinstatement of a decidedly ruthless sense of power presented a dilemma. Certainly mental health would not be served. Or would it? Could someone leading an amoral or even an immoral life be healthy? Whose standards should be used? When a person expressed belief in a given moral code, the Christian code for example, it was reasonable to judge him in accordance. But what about the atheist? What about the man whose conduct went ungoverned by a canonical restraint? Of course the mores of his social context might be used. But what if even these had been supplanted by a nonconforming lifestyle, a lifestyle such as Julian's? What was right and wrong for a youth like him? What was healthy?

This brand of query had visited Sister Zoë throughout her long career, but seldom with such vehemence. She acknowledged the necessity of doubt for building a durable faith—which hers had proven to be. Still, doubt shook things. Her bones, sometimes, felt brittle.

Faith was better based, perhaps, for it thrived on all those things she knew she did not know.

Being the only school-aged patient at St. Francis, Marcy posed an education problem. Sister Dana had done her best to fill the void, but at last conceded her skills were insufficient. Marcy's mind was too inquisitive. So it was decided that specific subjects, taught by whomever among the staff would volunteer, should supplement the youngster's general tutoring. Understandably this produced a curriculum rather heavy in psychology and religion. A plea was therefore made among the patients. And much to Sister Zoë's surprise, the response was overwhelming. Soon a schedule was worked out wherein Marcy's days (including many of her evenings) were largely to consist of shuttling from one course to another. The biggest surprise of all, however, was Julian's proposal to teach the young girl chess.

This change in Julian's attitude, i.e. his willingness to get involved, was most encouraging. Thus Sister Zoë was disposed to reconsider and to lift her ban.

Pending Marcy's approval, then, it was agreed that Julian's class would meet twice weekly, on Tuesdays and Fridays from two to three in the afternoon. The sanitarium's only chess set (plastic pieces and a red-black checkerboard) was promptly commandeered, whereupon

Julian unexpectedly produced his own beautifully hand-carved set. He suggested that the humbler one be given to his student so she would have the means to study and to practice.

Unlike most of the other courses—which were to be held in their instructors' rooms or offices—Julian's was assigned to the recreation hall. The nun was not particularly suspicious of his motives, but thought a modest caution to be well advised.

* * *

The hall was hollow and impersonal. It echoed dismally, mostly with the irritating click of ping-pong balls. Julian scouted out the least offensive spot—a semi-partitioned corner—to which he carried a card table and two folding chairs. From a felt-lined case he took out his chessmen. Their elegance, in the midst of such banality, was too incongruous. He put them back, setting up the plastic ones instead. It was 1:45 pm.

He waited. A gaggle of bridge-players shuffled cards nearby. Pool balls broke. The crass linoleum reverberated with recreating feet. Smokers fouled the air.

He tried to withdraw, to edit distractions, to find the

inner refuge he had lost—his meadow. It would not come. He stood and paced, ill-temperedly, slapping his soles down on the glossy floor. He sat again. It was worthless, this bid to gain the confidence of a mere adolescent—a pawn whose chances were slim to none of ever reaching the queening square. Why bother? What could possibly be in it for him… besides the win? He lowered his nose to the tabletop and peered out through the ranks. White vs. Black. Papp vs. Zoë. He could almost visualize a habit mantling the hostile King, the King in drag. Perversely, he found the image fitting.

'Hello.'

Marcy arrested his reverie. He rose.

'Am I late?'

It was their first meeting since they had mutually astounded one another with their fits. Marcy was inordinately nervous. Julian was simply irritated.

'These conditions are unbearable. Do you mind if we move?'

She looked around, not really understanding his objection. It was, after all, just a game they were going to play. But he was the teacher. She deferred.

'No, I don't mind. Where to?'

'My room.'

She balked.

'You needn't worry. I don't bite—except my tongue from time to time.'

'I don't think Sister Zoë would like it.'

'I'm sure not. But if I'm to teach you anything about "The Game of Games," peace and quiet are essential.'

She still hesitated.

'Tell you what, you run along to ole Ms. Zoë to get permission, and, if you get it, make sure she writes you a little note and pins it to your blouse. I'll be in my room, east wing, second floor, "suite" nine.'

He gathered up the sets and walked away. Marcy followed. At the double doors she stopped, watching as he crossed the common to see if he would look back. He did not. Not once. All the way. She knew he was trying to intimidate her into doing what he wanted. Sister had warned her that he was clever. She had also said the chess classes were optional. All the classes were, in fact, but Julian's in particular. And if Julian did anything to make her feel uncomfortable, she was to excuse herself and go straight to Sister Zoë. That seemed a bit extreme, however. He had been mean that first time, true, but he had just suffered one of his seizures; Sister had explained about those. She had also said that Julian seemed better, since a seizure had not happened in a while, and that his teaching offer was another healthy sign. Then there was what the Miniature Man had said—and the question of the poisoned pawn.

When Marcy reached his room the door was open. Julian obviously was expecting her, which made her mad.

He sat in a straight-backed chair at a little table, a second chair placed opposite. The board and chessmen were beautiful. She was instantly reminded of the Miniature Man, for the pieces each looked startlingly real. And though a lot of them were exactly alike in shape and size, no face was carved the same. Even the short ones (the pawns, she guessed), which outnumbered all the rest, were clearly individuals. Absorbed with their enchanting features, her pique at being "predictable" soon dissolved. She took the seat awaiting her.

Julian took no notice she was there. She found his reflective glasses rather irksome. They really made it impossible to tell where he was looking. Yet now that she was sitting right in front of him, she somehow knew his eyes were not on her. She utilized the interim to re-inspect the figures. They were all lined up like soldiers on parade—two separate armies facing each other with a frozen expectation, poised to be engaged by the touch of a human hand.

Like a striking snake, Julian's arm shot forward. Marcy flinched. When her heart stopped pounding she saw he had merely pushed a pawn to another square.

'You scared me.'

'Chess is a game of peremptory advantage. Your fear gives me the edge, just as would your inattention, lack of confidence, poor imagination. In other words, any flaw you carry to the board.'

'But I don't even know how to play.'

'One flaw, I trust, we'll soon amend. Tell me what you do know.'

She looked down at the board.

'I know these short ones are the pawns. And the tall ones are the King and Queen.'

'That's all?'

His question was dispassionate. It told her nothing of how he felt about her nearly total ignorance of the game. She tried, by way of compensating, to hazard some assumptions.

'All the pieces line up with each other at the start… A pawn can jump two squares at once.'

'On its first move only.'

'Oh.'

Within three-quarters of an hour, Marcy knew considerably more.

'You haven't mentioned the poisoned pawn.'

He sat back in his chair, bemused.

'Where did you hear that term?'

'Tell me what it is first.'

'It's a reference to the twenty-ninth move in the second game of the 1972 World Chess Championship—Spaasky vs. Fischer.'

She looked perplexed.

'You asked; I told you. So where did you hear it?'

'What does it mean, though?'

He paused a moment, then using the crisp, aggressive moves he consistently made with the chessmen, he set up the position.

'This won't mean much to you yet, but here's how things looked before that move. It's about even. Black could play for a draw but instead does this.'

He snatched the King Rook's pawn with the Bishop.

'After that the game was lost.' He held up the captured piece. 'That's why this was called "the poisoned pawn". By taking it, Fischer killed his chances. Most think it was the worst blunder of his career.'

Marcy thought a minute. Her ambivalence toward Sister Dana was disturbing. And since the courses had begun, the nun's behavior confused her even more. Yesterday she had escorted Marcy to every single class, was with her every second in between, asking how things went, whether she liked the teacher, checking assignments, offering help, hovering like a bee. Today, she knew, would have been the same, had Sister Zoë not intervened. And Marcy was glad she had. But why? Sister Dana was her closest friend, her only friend, really. Why, then, was she so relieved to be spared the nun's loving company?

'And was it?'

'Was it what?'

'"The worst blunder of his career"?'

'Who knows? It may have been a genuine flash of brilliance. Though if it was, he didn't follow through.'

'You mean he could have won?'

'If the move was based on what he saw, not on what he didn't. Why? Does this really make any sense to you?'

'No. No, you're right. Not yet.'

Julian pointed to the plastic chess set on the bed.

'That's for you, if you're interested enough to practice. I'm going to give you a chess problem every class. They're like riddles—and, when you understand them, poems.'

He cleared his own set, and motioned Marcy to open hers.

'As I call out the positions, you place the pieces. There's a simple notation system I'll show you so you won't have to memorize everything.'

She caught on quickly, and without much difficulty reproduced the problem from his symbols.

'It's White's turn. If the proper moves are made, Black is mated in two. The play is forced, which means that White's first move necessitates Black's reply, White's second move causing Mate. Understand?'

'I think so.'

'Well, I don't expect you to solve it anyway. It's just to help you get familiar with the way each piece moves.'

'I'll solve it.'

'Your confidence is charming, but don't count on it. You barely know a Bishop from a Rook.'

'I'll solve it.'

He laughed.

'Class dismissed.'

Marcy focused one last look at the position, gathered up the pieces, and closed the notation slip between the covers of the folding checkerboard.

'See you Friday… Julian? Or Mr. Papp?'

'If you solve the problem—Julian. Otherwise, it's Mr. Papp.'

'Friday, then, Mr. Papp. And thanks.'

'My pleasure.'

He saw her out, shutting the door behind her.

How well it had gone! His gambit for location seemed successful, for when Ms. Zoë was told the class had proceeded without incident, he doubted she would take issue with the change. The girl apparently enjoyed herself. In fact, she had been enthusiastic. Coupling that to her ready comprehension (not to mention that Julian found her rather likeable), the teaching part might not be such a drag. And most important of all, she had relaxed. She seemed to trust him. No doubt about it, the climate for The Game's commencement could not be more favorable.

* * *

A knock on Marcy's door received no answer. Sister Dana slipped inside. Marcy sat at her writing desk, poring over the problem "Papp" had set her. She had dropped the "Mr." an hour before, having found what she believed was the first key move. Since then she had checked and double-checked and triple-checked the alternatives ad nauseam. This *had* to be the move. It was the only one that forced Black's play. But where was Mate? No matter how airtight each trap appeared, the swarthy King escaped.

'Damn!'

'Marcy!'

The girl jumped.

'Sister Dana! I didn't hear you come in.'

'Obviously not. That was not a very seemly word.'

'No, sorry. But this is driving me bananas. Do you know anything about this game?'

'Afraid not. What's got you so upset?'

'Homework.'

'In chess? Aren't your other subjects more important?'

'I finished all of them.'

The nun looked down over Marcy's shoulder.

'What do you have to do?'

'Mate the Black King. In two moves. Which isn't as easy as it sounds.'

'Why would Julian start you out with such a difficult problem?'

'Just meanness, I suppose.'

'Marcy!'

'I'm only kidding. He said he didn't think I'd work it out. But just because of that I'm going to. If it kills me.'

'How long have you been at it?'

'Hours!'

'Don't you think it's time to take a break then? You can only concentrate on a thing so long. Come on. Get those clothes off and climb into bed. It's nearly midnight.'

She gently pulled Marcy's chair away from the desk.

'Maybe you're right. I'll probably get it all figured out and Friday he'll tell me it's wrong, that one of these pieces can jump in some new stupid way.'

'Well, I wouldn't worry about it. It's only a game.'

'Not the way Julian plays it—Mr. Papp, I mean.'

'He makes you call him "Mr. Papp"?'

'Unless I solve the problem. Isn't that mean?'

Secretly Sister Dana was pleased at Julian's disfavor. She disliked like him. She also distrusted him—especially around Marcy. Had he not already broken the rules by holding class up in his room? She had left her protest ringing in the ears of her superior (who had said she would attend to it). Had final word been Sister Dana's, the ban would have been promptly re-imposed.

What was wrong? Marcy had stopped unbuttoning her blouse. She was standing very still, just looking, waiting. For what? Then it struck the nun; she had not seen

Marcy nude in weeks, not totally, not since the bathing incident, for after that the girl had taken charge herself of private needs. The nun drew back. What might have been perceived as a normal adolescent modesty, instead became a stinging accusation. Why was she standing there like that? What could the girl be thinking? How dare her eyes be filled with such reproach! A seething guilt assailed the nun, an all-consuming shame. She flushed. She could not speak. And fearing she could never-ever face the girl again, she fled the room.

* * *

'Good morning, Mr. Papp.'

'Ms. Zoë.'

'How good of you to come.'

'More so than any other morning?' He downed the pills. 'Just came for my fix.'

'And is the medication working?'

'Some. No fits, at least.'

'Any side effects?'

'Still want to puke at times, but I can stand it.'

'Sleeping?'

'No. That all?'

'Oh, please, sit down.'

He did.

'You have that Father Confessor look, Ms. Zoë. I warn you, it's been seven years since my last confession. How's your stamina?'

'I merely want to ask you how your chess class went with Marcy. Did you find her a competent student?'

'Too soon to tell. She's quick enough. Retention is the question.'

'I don't think she'll disappoint you there.'

'Good memory?'

'For the most part, yes.'

'But not always.'

'No. She does forget sometimes.'

'Memory is a funny mechanism—"fickle". For instance, Marcy asked me yesterday about a chess term she'd heard somewhere. She had no idea what it meant. But it jogged my memory so much I've been up with it half the night.'

'I don't think I…'

'No, you couldn't; I'll explain. It concerned a famous championship. After Marcy left I reconstructed one of its best-known games, and before I knew what happened I'd played all twenty. Odd, isn't it, how the tiniest fragment will reactivate whole episodes? How's your memory, Ms. Zoë?'

'Sometimes I think more feeble than fickle, certainly

compared to one like yours. Do you remember everything, or just those things in which you're interested?'

'It's all accessible. You'd be surprised what I can pull, even from the cradle. Very Oedipal. I shouldn't say "all," though. There are a few impressions that "lurk un-retrieved." It's like they're waiting for me to find some novel means of understanding, as if they're so removed from my immediate experience that nothing I ordinarily envision describes them. I think forgetting certain dreams is a similar phenomenon. If something totally unfamiliar happens in our sleep, something that defies associations, chances are we'll lose it once awake—the result of being programmed by a literal reality.'

'You've apparently thought about this a great deal.'

'Of course. When your mind is the repository for every piddling bit of information, it's natural to wonder how and why. Are you familiar with categorization?'

'If you mean the mind's ability to store and classify things, yes.'

'I guess that's apt. In some of my exhibitions I play as many as ten games simultaneously. Each one merely occupies its own niche in my head. I just skip from board to board, making the respective moves. It's a terrific stunt. Tends to mystify the uninitiated. But actually, it's no big deal. Everybody can do it to some extent. Marcy, for example.'

'Oh?'

'You said she forgets selectively.'

'Did I?'

'Her mind obviously is categorizing. Anything she chooses not to remember, she stores in a special niche—the one with the gatekeeper.'

'Gatekeeper?'

The Miniature Man, of course, which Julian left unstated. He felt he had said enough already, enough to serve notice formally: The Game had begun.

'Just a pet theory of mine, Ms. Zoë. I should thank you, by the way.'

'For what?'

'Well, I realize the emphasis Catholics place on good appearances, and how, on the surface, Marcy's coming to my room might be misread. So I thank you for braving public opinion in deference to my class's need for privacy. The recreation hall—though charming—is simply not conducive to the concentration chess demands.'

'I'm afraid I may have to disappoint you on that score, Mr. Papp. Though appearances do often belie intentions, an argument can also be made for substance following form. Our diverse population warrants a degree of liberality, but the privacy of which you speak is stretching things… Unless you would be willing to expand your class to include more pupils? A number of people have expressed an interest.'

'Out of the question.'

'I think we ought to resume, then, the original agreement.'

'I'd have no objection to a chaperone. Ms. Clara might oblige.'

'Well that's a thought. She's very busy, but I can certainly ask her. Or someone else. Come to think of it, Sister Dana might be more available.'

'Whomever.'

* * *

Wednesday, October 29th, at 11:10 in the A.M. I overslept and almost missed my Ancient History class. Mr. Jimmy scolded me. He wasn't angry, though. He's sad. I think he only wants someone to talk to. He told me all about New Hampshire where he grew up, and how the fall always makes him think of picking apples. He's been here a long, long time. He's very old.

The reason I didn't wake up in time was Sister Dana. I couldn't sleep thinking about her. Last night her feelings got hurt because I didn't want to get undressed in front of her. I don't know why I didn't. She's seen me before. I just felt embarrassed, not having any hair, and with all my ugly red marks. So I waited for her to turn around. Instead she ran away. I think she was crying. Lately she's been acting really strange.

I know what a poisoned pawn is now. Julian told me. But I'm not too sure how it applies to Sister Dana. I'll have to wait and see.

***

The water was intentionally scalding; the straight razor fogged with steam. The patterned tile pressed octagonal prints into the skin of penitent knees... as Sister Dana prayed:

'Dear Father, I have grievously sinned in mind and body. I am unworthy to address Thee. I love. But my love is tainted. Pleasures of the flesh have sullied it before Thine eyes and made it base and contemptible. For I am weak. Lust contaminates my blood. I must abuse myself to staunch its carnal flow. Yet still these unchaste thoughts persist. I cannot beg forgiveness, Lord; it is too undeserved.

'I know I will sin again. I must. But help me, Father, help me. The one I love is blameless. She is good and pure and would not stoop to cravings such as mine. My only fear is that she will find me out and come to hate me. That I could not bear. I cannot change the way I am, but Marcy need not know. I thought I saw it in her eyes. I thought her innocence accused me.

'But maybe not. Maybe I imagined it. Maybe there is still time to prove my love for her is not profane. Please, Lord; please do not take her from me. I promise never to let my secret defile her. I swear it. I will protect her always from myself, as well as from all others. I will, dear Lord, I will. I will, I swear it.'

The nun crossed herself and rose. She stepped one foot, then the other—numbly—into the seething tub. A heat rash blossomed instantly on her ankles, calves, and knees, bleeding upward. She closed her eyes. Her nostrils flared, breathing in the vapor. The pain she blocked with her mind still registered in her crooked fingers. She clenched her teeth. Then, legs spread out as widely as the confining tub sides allowed, she slowly squatted.

The agony was nearly overpowering. It ravaged deeply, blistering the tender skin, withering the folds like leaves on fire. Her eyes streamed tears. Her lungs felt fearfully constrained. She swallowed hard, again and again, as if to keep contained her seething dose of suffering.

Then stoically she soaped herself, working up lather in her lap. She grasped the razor. It had belonged to her father's father, then to him, passed on to her—a keepsake she had coveted from the day he died. She had kept it sharp, well stropped, and ready. It was with this she had shaved her scalp. It was with this she now removed what hair remained.

* * *

It's growing! I can hardly believe it! I was brushing my teeth, looking in the mirror, and there it was! Hair! I almost swallowed the suds. There's not much, of course. You have to look real close. But there are hundreds, thousands probably. I'm going to be normal! I wanted to run and show Sister Zoë and Sister Dana and all my tutors, even Julian. But then I decided it would be more fun to wait and see. I have English, Math, and Chess today, three chances for people to notice. It's 7:22 in the A.M., thirty-eight minutes until my first class. I'm going to look in the mirror some more. I'm a brunette!

* * *

The nuns, both clad in heavy woollen sweaters, walked side by side. Their breath hung visibly in the chilly autumn air. They had done one turn of the frost-dusted grounds in silence. On this, their second, they spoke.

'I've talked to Julian. I believe his objection to the rec hall is legitimate. It does tend to be rather loud.'

'You haven't given in to him, I hope!'

'I question your choice of words, Sister Dana, but I have agreed to let him hold his classes in his room.'

'Sister!'

'Chaperoned, of course.'

'Oh... He agreed to that?'

'Why wouldn't he?'

She ignored the question.

'But who?'

'Julian suggested Sister Clara.'

'He would. Of course. The next best thing to being by themselves.'

The old nun's dubious look bade the younger to explain.

'She'll fall asleep! You know it's true. She's always nodding off. I don't mean to be unkind but, with Sister Clara on guard, Marcy just isn't safe.'

'Safe? From what?'

'From him, of course. He may look innocent to you, but it's crystal-clear to me what's on his mind.'

'Which is?'

'Oh, come now, Sister Zoë, don't be naïve. Do I have to spell it out for you?'

'I think you better had.'

'S-E-X, Sister. Sex is all he's after. Any fool can see that.' She saw that her zeal had carried her too far. 'I'm sorry, Sister. Really, I apologize... But don't you see how obvious it is?'

'I guess I don't. You haven't mentioned this in any of your reports. Unless you've omitted something?'

'Oh, no. It's only a feeling.'

'Well, perhaps you'd be less worried if the job of

chaperone were yours.'

At first this prospect frightened Sister Dana. She had yet to reconcile herself to Marcy. It was too soon. She was not ready. Then, suddenly, the situation looked ideal! How better to inaugurate the protective role she had vowed to play?

'That is, Sister, if you have the time.'

'Two to three on Tuesdays and Fridays?'

'I believe that's right.'

'I think I can... Yes, I'm sure. It won't be any trouble.'

'Then you don't mind?'

'No. Well, yes. I mean, most likely it will be a bore. Unless I learn the silly game myself. You don't suppose he'd teach us both?'

'No, I think not. Marcy is an exception as it is, I understand. Julian has never taught. His mother was quite shocked the day I told her.'

'You called her?'

'She called me—and has, every other day, for weeks. I tried to discourage her early on, gently, but to no avail. Now I think, without the frequent contact, her fear that she has abandoned Julian would grow to be intolerable. I was so grateful the other day to have something new to tell her, I'm afraid I sort of blurted it out. There was a long silence on the line—which held I know not what—followed by her effusive thanks for all that we were doing for her son, the gist of which made plain that Julian never before had considered taking on a student; had, in fact, disparaged the idea.'

'You see? I told you he had something else in mind.'

'We disagree, however, on what that is.'

'Okay, what do you believe he's up to?'

'As I said, I think there are many things involved, not the least of which is Julian's need to justify his existence. His suicide attempts were in response to a specific crisis. That crisis is over, leaving him to confront the situation, one his fears have him convinced is a hopeless void— which he now must fill. Undertaking Marcy as a project or a challenge is a life-sustaining enterprise for Julian. So, whether you judge his conscious motives honorable or otherwise, I trust you will keep their vital source in mind. Watch, protect if necessary, but do not interfere.'

The young nun knew debate was closed, that "policy" had been made.

'Yes, Sister. Should I continue my reports?'

'Once weekly should be sufficient.'

'Unless?'

'Unless, of course, you note some telling change.'

They parted, walking off to their respective tasks.

* * *

Thus far, no one had noticed. Marcy had checked the mirror after each of her morning classes to verify that her hair was really there. It was. So why was everyone so blind? True, she had not seen Sister Zoë or Sister Dana yet, but there were others who might have marked the change. Maybe people failed to look at those labeled "different." Maybe people's habit of pretending (through politeness, or compassion, or their own embarrassment) that everything—even hairlessness—was normal, prevented them from actually seeing.

After her initial disappointment, Marcy had begun to watch. Sure enough the eyes she met, more often than not, were averted—at least when she tried to engage them. Those with whom she had stopped to talk would look in her direction, but their vision somehow failed to take her in. She had to laugh at all the times she had fretted over stares. People gawk, but now she knew they seldom see.

So, by the time she arrived for chess class, Marcy had renounced her expectations.

His door was open. Julian waited at the table. The problem he had assigned her was set on the board. He stood this time as Marcy entered.

'Good afternoon, Mr. Papp.'

He smiled (that nasty smirk of his).

'I see.'

She hated that she had failed to solve the problem (almost as much as admitting it to him).

'I tried.'

'I'm sure you did.'

His condescension galled her even more. She took her seat.

He pointed head-ward.

'Been watering up there?'

She blushed crimson—not from bashfulness, but from joy. He had noticed! Somebody had noticed! For that one minute, she loved him with all her heart. She felt he was sincerely glad for her—despite the wryness of his quip—because his second smile was not a smirk at all. It was warm and friendly and therefore worthy of sharing this remarkable event.

Huffing and puffing, Sister Dana hurriedly marched in. Julian resumed his seat.

'Sister! What are you doing here?'

The nun looked around self-consciously. Both chairs being taken, there was nowhere left to sit except on the bed. She held her ground.

'Didn't he tell you?'

'Tell me what?'

Julian explained.

'She's to be your bodyguard whenever you cross the threshold of my lair. Welcome, Ms. Dana, pull up a chair—sounds rather lyric—oh, but there isn't a spare. The bed, my bed, my lonely bed, beckons if you dare.'

'I didn't come here to be ridiculed, Julian.'

'Mr. Papp.'

'*Sister* Dana.'

Noting the stress in Marcy's face, Julian changed his tone.

'Well, now that we're all reacquainted, won't you please sit down?'

The room had been rearranged to put as much space as possible between the bed and chairs.

Having little choice, Sister Dana took the seat offered.

Satisfied (for the moment) with the relative positions, Julian proceeded to teach his lesson. He asked that Marcy show him how she had worked toward the solution, checking the precision of her moves. She knew the pieces well enough. *En passant* was what she had forgotten. He reviewed it for her, then left the problem unsolved.

'But what's the answer?'

'You'll get it now. But do it later.'

'Same deal?'

'My name, you mean?'

She nodded.

'Sure, same deal.'

They moved on to various mating exercises whereby Marcy was to trap his King with hers plus one or two other pieces. She thought these drills great fun and lost herself to the rigors of the chase.

Meanwhile Sister Dana brooded. Julian's reformed behavior seemingly neutralized her role, made it look superfluous, even silly. Her presence was an imposition—or so she felt it was perceived. And her gnawing pain of isolation was worsened by the exclusivity of Marcy's concentration.

As the nun observed, the afternoon sun poured in through the bedroom window, framing the couple, enshrining their heads in a pair of fuzzy halos.

Marcy's head! The nun almost cried out. Her skin flushed hot, yet at the same time she felt cold. The time to spontaneously express her joy for Marcy quickly lapsed. Now the words were paralyzed (if, indeed, they had ever formed).

Sister Zoë. She must report to Sister Zoë. Unsteadily the young nun found her feet.

'Check.'

He moved away.

'Check.'

He moved again.

'Check!'

Again he eluded her.

Marcy puffed out her cheeks in consternation.

'I don't have enough material.'

'That's right.'

She cocked her head sideways and threw him a petulant look.

'Then why have you let me chase you all over the place, knowing I couldn't mate you?'

'Because I listed for you on Tuesday the minimum forces needed for a win. Had you recalled, you would have known ten minutes ago that two Knights and a King were insufficient.'

'You expect me to remember everything.'

'That's my goal.'

'I think that's unfair. Besides, I was nervous last time.'

'Oh?'

'What do you mean, "Oh?" Weren't you?'

'No.'

'Well, I was. And I don't remember good when I'm nervous.'

'Remember *well*.'

'Remember *well*.'

'You're doing all right—better than I expected.'

'Because you thought I was stupid.'

'I denied that before; I deny it again.'

'Don't underestimate me, Mr. Papp. If you teach me "well," I'll beat you at this game some day.'

'You'll never beat me, Marcy.'

He said it as simply and with as much conviction as one might assert that the sky was blue.

She looked at his face, toward his eyes, trying to pierce the darkness that concealed them.

'Why do you wear those?'

'My eyes are hypersensitive to the light.'

'You wear them at night, too.'

'I wear them at night, too.'

'Why?'

'Who's the Miniature Man?'

With this question her eyes refocused—and in the polished black of his impenetrable lenses she saw her own reflection. It gave her an odd feeling, a sort of hum at the base of her skull, a deep vibration that was at once pleasurable and frightening. For a moment she let herself indulge in its lulling frequency, allowing it to open an unfamiliar channel—through which Julian's question droningly resounded: Who *was* the Miniature Man? By a wrenching dint of will, she broke the spell.

'I don't think I want to tell you.'

'I don't think you know.'

He was right; she didn't. Perhaps she didn't want to know, not yet. But what could Julian know about it? She considered his presumptuousness rather insulting.

'Let's stick to chess.'

'It wasn't I who changed the subject.'

'Well it certainly wasn't…'

He indicated his glasses.

'Oh, it was… Sorry.' She looked away. 'Hey, where's Sister Dana? I forgot she was even here.'

'Thus is no longer—quite a knack you have.'

'Huh?'

'Nothing.'

"Where do you suppose she went?"

'To take a leak, perhaps. Or don't nuns pee?'

She glowered at him.

'I don't blame her for leaving. You weren't very nice to her.'

'Why should I be nice to the opposition's emissary?'

'The what? Whose?'

'Ms. Zoë's.'

'Why do you call her that?'

'The opposition?'

'No, "Ms."'

'Oh, just a token of disrespect. While feminism hasn't cracked the "God-fearing" mentalities, one does one's best to promulgate the cause.'

Marcy was unsure if he was kidding or sincere.

'But Sister Zoë is a nun.'

'And that's her problem. When ultimately women see that sexism infests religion, they'll move to halt the bunk's proliferation.'

This was a bit abstruse for Marcy, although she caught his drift.

'I don't understand then what you're doing here. At St. Francis, I mean.'

'Ask my mother.'

'She *made* you come?'

'Let's say she pressed a dutiful advantage. I wasn't thinking very clearly at the time. And when one shows weakness, the initiative is quickly seized by others—thus depositing me here.'

'You mean against your will?'

'Well, no.'

The truth was, no one at St. Francis was under obligation to remain (except for Marcy, whose status as a minor raised a legal issue). This non-compulsory policy afforded the Order considerable leeway in such things as acceptance of its patients, methods of their treatment, and the circumstances determining their release. Belligerents and malcontents were seldom tolerated. If such predispositions were detected on admission, or if they surfaced later, a patient was rejected or removed. Exceptions could be made, of course, and were. But contrary behaviors had to improve (improve significantly) if their authors hoped to guarantee their stay. And if a patient left without permission, reentry was forever barred. It was generally understood, then, that one responded to treatment positively at St. Francis, or one sought treatment elsewhere.

Julian was readily aware of this contingency and knew his abusive attitude, his contempt for regulations, and his outspoken irreverence for the nuns put him at risk. He likewise was aware the sanitarium did have benefits to offer. Tangibly, the natural setting, the peaceful isolation, the relative anonymity he enjoyed, were all considerations. Intangibly (and thus harder to articulate), a vague impression had somewhere dawned that things—

fundamentally significant things—were in the offing.

He looked intently at the girl before him: fuzzy crown, lively eyes, fair skin tones, lollipop lips—intelligent features wed in a conspiracy of youth and guilelessness. No, it was not against his will that he was here, not any longer.

'Does your mother visit you?'

'Not allowed.'

'Really? That doesn't sound right. The other patients…'

'I forbade her.'

'Oh… Don't you get along?'

'My mother suffers from the lifelong delusion that the two of us get along famously. Nothing short of matricide would change her mind. I, on the other hand, view our present arrangement—"pals" with a countrywide buffer—as immeasurably agreeable. Which isn't to say I dislike the woman. She's supported me unselfishly from the day I was born, making, I might add, a most remarkable transition from parent to patron. Had she not kept me sheltered from a mercenary world, my talent never would have been developed. Owing her that, I owe her everything. But gratitude, at times, deserves a rest.'

Marcy paused to take this in, for sometimes his vocabulary had her stumped. She wondered at understanding him at all. And yet she did. Despite the unfamiliar words, the convoluted sentences, despite her slight suspicion that he *wanted* to confuse her, she nonetheless believed she understood him. And she appreciated the fact that he refused to talk down to her.

'What about your father?'

'Officially a Missing Person. What about yours?'

She faltered.

'I—he's…'

'Dead?'

'No!'

She tried to think. Who were her parents? Why did they have no names, no faces? How could "mother," "father," "sister," "brother" be empty terms?

Her eyes grown wide, she gaped at Julian, his glasses again twin mirrors. No, not dead, she mouthed the words. But what then? Lost? No answers came. Only Marcy's tears—as much from frustration as from despair.

'Stop it!'

Julian's shout so startled her she obeyed.

'What gives you the right to yell at me?'

'Only your self-pity. It's maudlin. Your faulty memory is what's made you an orphan. Jar that and I'm sure you'll find a pair of doting parents waiting.'

'You think so? You really do?'

'Of course. Do you think you were brought here by the stork, dropped down from its beak all bald and bawling, a helpless babe at age "fourteen?" Grow up, kid. Your hair is.'

'But I honestly don't remember certain things.'

'I know.'

'Then how is it my fault?'

'I said "faulty memory," not that the forgetting was your fault.'

'I've tried remembering.'

He looked unimpressed.

'I have! Sister Zoë even hypnotized me.'

'And didn't get past your Miniature Man.'

Marcy suddenly was angry.

'How do you know? What do you know about anything anyway? If Sister can't make me remember, *you* sure won't be able to.'

'Not against your will.'

'That's right!'

She was almost screaming at him. He waited, allowing her to grasp the irony in what she had just let slip. But she was much too busy hating him to stop and think of anything beyond retaliation. A flash of intuition came. It galvanized Marcy's hand. With a well-aimed flick she toppled Julian's King.

Neither made a move.

Marcy sensed his awful, unseen eyes bore into her. His face remained unnervingly composed. Then, with a motion made so slowly she felt it as a mortal threat, Julian reached and righted the fallen King.

'Class dismissed.'

'Is she aware?'

'I don't know. I was going to say something but…'

'But?'

'I didn't want to interrupt their class.'

'How did that go, by the way?'

'Well, being watched, of course he behaved himself where Marcy was concerned. He was rude to me, though.'

'Don't take that too personally. He's rude to everyone. How about Marcy?'

'I guess she's learning. From what I could see, he's awfully demanding.'

'So he *is* teaching her the game.'

'Yes.'

'And enjoying it himself?'

'I wouldn't know. His back was to me most of the time so I couldn't tell.'

'He didn't include you in any way?'

'"*In*clude me"? He did everything he could to *ex*clude me. I had to sit all by myself on the opposite side of the room and watch them both pretend I wasn't there.'

'How unpleasant for you. I'm sorry. If you'd like, perhaps I could find somebody else.'

'No, Sister, thank you. I'll just remember to take along a book next time, or some paperwork.'

Sister Zoë glanced at her watch.

'Marcy is between classes now. Would you mind asking her to come and see me?'

'What about her hair? Should I say anything?'

'Why don't you wait until I've talked with her.'

'Yes, Sister.'

The nun excused herself and left.

Marcy, however, was nowhere to be found. Sister Dana checked her room, the rec hall, the cafeteria, the library, the chapel, checked with all of Marcy's tutors. Nobody had seen her after Julian—who claimed she had left his room at three o'clock. The nun began to worry. By dinnertime, and still no Marcy, she was frantic. Even Sister Zoë expressed concern. Julian was asked again if anything had happened to upset the girl. He had answered with a terse and uncommunicative 'No.'

MELANIE

It was dark. It was cold. The moon shone dimly, a tallowy glow through clouds like frosted glass. Tree limbs shivered. Evergreens looked massive. The ground was brittle with frozen fallen leaves. Marcy sat at the edge of a clearing, motionlessly alone. Her eyes were closed, her back—supported by an aspen trunk—was braced against the night.

The mismatched eyes blinked open.

'You!'

They disappeared in a wincing mass of wrinkles, hands clapped over ears.

Realizing her mistake, Marcy tried to make amends in

mime. He looked at her mistrustfully.

You're going to behave?

She nodded.

No more booming timpani?

She shook her head.
Cautiously he lowered his hands.

**Well. I was about to say how nice it was to see you—
before the din.**

She moved to apologize again, but he waved her off.

**What brings you here this fine October eve; trick or
treat?**

Huh?

**Never mind. Just need a friend, I'll wager. Julian not
much help?**

He's awful!

Marcy's predetermined plan, when next she met the
Miniature Man, had been to ask specific questions. His
unexpected appearance, however, chased that plan away.
She found herself caught up in the immediate situation,
conducting herself accordingly, as if this dream or vision or

hallucination—whatever it was—had its own inviolable dynamic.

Make fun of that new crop of peach-fuzz you've sprouted, did he?

With a shy but happy smile she ran her palm across her scalp, relishing its stubbly feel.

No?

No. He was nice about my hair.

The old man's face was illuminated in a yellow flash of match light as he lit his pipe and puffed an acrid cloud of smoke. Watching as it swirled and eddied, Marcy grew aware of her surroundings. She was once again inside the chamber with its walls of antique books, the stove crackling loudly in one corner, sawdust coating everything, as usual—except his tools, which lay in wait near a thumb-high pile of fresh shavings.

What, then?

He was at me about my past again.

Persistent fellow. Tell him anything?

How could I, when I don't remember?

Nothing about your parents?

No.

Or about your older sisters?

No.

The embers in his pipe bowl glowed.

Wait. Do I have sisters?

Two.

But how do you know that?

I know everything that you know. Maybe a little more.

The specific questions she was going to ask returned. She shaped her lips to form the first.

Who are you?

I believe I've been dubbed the Miniature Man and the Gatekeeper, so far. I'll answer to either.

But who are you really?

Maybe you'd care to conjure up another name for me—

one from a time when those budding curls hung well down 'twixt your shoulders?

She focused on the sculptor's hands, their jutting veins like pathways, routes she once had traced with tiny fingers...

'Benjamin!'

The night air reproduced his name in a breath of moonlit vapor. It lingered momentarily before her now wide-open eyes, then vanished—as did all of its vital connotations.

Marcy stood, knees gone stiff from the cold, wondering where she was, peering into the darkness all around as if in search of something, someone. Who? She tried to think. Him. A man. Whose name was… Benjamin. At least that much she had retained. But all else now was lost in her concern to find the way that she had come. She tried to get her bearings. The clearing. Had she crossed it to take up her position underneath the tree? No. She turned. The moon withdrew its cloud-diluted aid and blackness fell. Uncertain of each step, she picked her way. Fear of the dark. She mustn't let it gain the upper hand.

Then blessedly the night resounded. It was the chapel bell. It kept on ringing—twelve, thirteen, fourteen—as if it were conscious of being Marcy's guide. She followed it, and soon was safely home.

'You gave us quite a fright, young lady.'

'Sorry, Sister.'

'Where did you go?'

'For a walk. A long walk. I had to think.'

'Troubles, Marcy?'

She nodded.

'Can I help?'

She paused in order to pull together her doubts, her apprehensions, giving them some comprehensive form.

'Why can't I remember, Sister Zoë?'

The nun had now to search herself for the most insightful way to answer. Was the girl prepared to brave a confrontation with her past? Was she strong enough? Secure enough? Had the weeks of tender care built a trustworthy foundation, on which, faced with the brutal truth, her patient could depend?

'We believe your loss of memory stems from a particular event, something to which you were subjected, something so upsetting that your mind has blocked it out.'

What? A part of her demanded to know. Yet she asked a different question.

'Why wouldn't I remember things before, though?'

'We can't be certain, but it is likely that the girl to whom this happened wanted so much for it not to be, she determined to erase it by forgetting who she was. If she could be an altogether different human being, she could tell herself that nothing bad had happened.'

'So it was "bad"—what happened to me?'

'It was bad. It was not your fault. But it was bad.'

Marcy thought some more.

'Julian was right, then.'

'Oh? What did he say?'

'That I could remember if I really wanted to. That's not exactly how he put it, but that's what it all meant.'

'What all?'

'Me getting mad. I was mean, too. I do want to remember, though. Part of me does. The part that knows Benjamin.'

'And who is Benjamin?'

'The Miniature Man. I know him—from the time before. When I was little… Sister, will you hypnotize me again?'

Was it this for which the nun had searched? Was this the key to an entryway that might avoid having to batter down the door?

'Let me go tell Sister Dana we will be a while. I think she's just outside.'

In the hall, Sister Dana was deep in prayer. Marcy's disappearance, she believed, had been a judgment. The Lord was finally punishing the young nun's sins. That His means, however, would harm an innocent, had raised embittered doubts about her Faith. A crisis had ensued from which the nun, no less than Marcy, had been rescued. In all humility, she now gave fervent thanks.

'Excuse me, Sister.'

The nun unclasped her hands.

'Marcy and I will be some time yet. Perhaps you had better say good night; see her in the morning.'

The young nun hesitated.

'Don't worry. She's all right. And I'll see to it she gets back to quarters safely.'

'Yes, Sister.'

The elder helped the younger with her coat, opened the outer door, and with a reassuring pat on the back dismissed her.

'Now then, Marcy. Comfortable?'

'Is she okay?'

'Yes, I think so. Sister Dana sometimes overreacts to things.'

'She was really worried, wasn't she?'

'She's very fond of you.'

'I know.'

'Well. Are you ready?'

'Uh huh.'

'Relax then... That's good... And picture the little door set in your forehead... how it opens... to the warm, soft light inside.'

The elevator took her quickly to the deepest level.

Back so soon?

She ran to him.

Leaning over, allowing her little arms to wrap themselves around his neck, he let her kiss him. He picked her up and set her in his lap. His marvelous hands arranged her flowing curls.

Have you been working hard, Benjamin?

I always work hard.

What have you been making?

Would you like to see?

Uh huh.

Can't.

Oh, please? Pretty please?

Pretty please indeed!

He scowled. He always scowled when Melanie used baby-talk.

It's not finished.

But can't I see so far?

Out of the question.

Well, okay then.

It was the game they played. He would say no. She would plead. He would get gruff. Then she would be set loose to wander until she found the niche in which his latest work was hiding. She disengaged his veiny arms and scrambled down to start her explorations.

As she went, she let her index finger plow a squiggly trail through the sawdust's thick accumulation. Former tracks—their ages corresponding to their faintness— wiggled off in all directions. And one by one she passed the cloistered worlds. Each had been her favorite until the newest overtook her fancy. This time was no exception.

A circus! On tiptoe, for the niche was placed above her head, she gazed delightedly at what Benjamin had made: lions and tigers and panthers and bears and elephants holding elephants' tails. She imagined she could hear the tuxedoed ringmaster introducing acts, the drum roll sounding, the clowns evoking squeals of laughter from a motley crowd. It was all so wonderful, so real! But what was missing? There was always a part that Benjamin left out—one it was up to her to find so she could hurry back and report his error. She looked more critically. The string of elephants had no gaps. The lion-tamer had his whip and chair. The human cannonball's net lay ready. The aerialists! From a slender thread a somersaulting woman hung suspended. But the trapeze she had left was the only one there. No one waited at another, with outstretched arms, prepared to catch her.

Triumphantly she marched back to her friend.

Melanie, what's up?

Boy, oh boy, Benjamin. You really goofed this time.

You think so, eh?

I sure do. Come with me.

She took him by the hand and led him down a dusky corridor. The tableau filled a pocket at its end. Once there she pointed to the hapless acrobat.

Now what do you suppose is going to happen to that poor girl when she stops spinning?

She'll probably fall and break her neck.

Benjamin! You're not going to let that happen, are you?

He held out his other hand. Its bulging knuckles indicated something inside. She eyed him knowingly. With mock resistance he let her pry his fingers from the prize. She, in turn, feigned great relief on seeing the tiny figure with the trapeze.

I should hope so.

Benjamin rigged the necessary threads and, lifting Melanie, let her hang the catcher by the crooks behind his knees. Still in his arms, she gazed upon his work with satisfaction, letting her child's imagination reanimate the scene.

* * *

Saturday, November 1st, at 8:22 in the A.M. My real name is Melanie. It came out last night. Everything started with Julian being nasty, and me taking a walk, and having a dream, and getting lost, and, thanks to Sister Dana, finding my way back home. Then Sister Zoë hypnotized me. She doesn't like to because I don't pay any attention to her instructions once I'm under. But the results were better this time. The Miniature Man is a friend of mine from when I was a child. His name is Benjamin. I visited him twice yesterday. Once in the dream, when I remembered who he was… (Oh! And that I have two sisters! I forgot that part. I'll have to tell Sister.)… and then again later. The second one is real clear. I was little and saw a circus and I had beautiful long brown hair, all the way to my bottom. I hope it'll be like that again. Right now my head looks kind of like a rotten peach—all brown and fuzzy. The hairs are growing, though. I checked in the mirror this morning and they were definitely longer.

Anyway, I don't know what my last name is, or anything about my sisters. But Melanie is a start. Everybody is supposed to call me that from now on. Which will be strange. I had gotten used to Marcy. I liked it better. Except of course that Melanie isn't bald.

* * *

Julian sat at the corner table in the dining area near the cafeteria's east windows, staring into his coffee cup, watching the milky whirlpool his spoon had stirred, waiting—as he did each morning—for his nine o'clock "doping". The drugs were causing fewer spells of nausea. Worse, however, were the disturbances to his sleep. Insomniac by nature, what repose he got was being infiltrated by a nightmare. At least he thought it was a nightmare, since he would awaken nightly in cold sweats, often horrified. Of what, he did not know. The experience recurred; it seemed identical each time, though nothing of it overlapped his consciousness. Under normal circumstances he had total recall. Yet this dream, whose aftershock was mauling him emotionally, eluded his remembering it completely. He only knew it viscerally, as a residue of fear—vulgar, sick, and fetid, like a scum on the skin.

He took a sip of coffee, holding it in his mouth, letting its heavy resins stain the surface of his tongue. He had made up his mind. He would have to tell "the pill-pusher" something, something convincing enough to get the foul prescription changed. Perhaps the truth would do. Not the whole truth, but an abridged version, leaving out the part about his fear, and his haunting sense that the dream was other then drug-induced.

He drained his cup and set it back inside its ring. There was The Game to consider, too.

'You're very punctual, Mr. Papp.'

'Disgusting, isn't it.'

'No, I'm most appreciative. In fact your visits have become a rather pleasant fixture in my day. So much so, that I find myself reluctant to suggest they be less frequent. It is time, though, don't you think, for you to take this medication by yourself?'

'The stuff's not working.'

'You've had another seizure?'

'No, it's the fucking side effects.'

'Could you describe them a little more articulately, Mr. Papp?'

'That says it. You've transformed me from a eunuch

into a sex fiend—non-corporeally speaking, that is.'

'You're having erotic urges?'

'Experiences, Ms. Zoë, experiences—though they're not all that "erotic". And they happen in my sleep, so you can quell that excommunicatory zeal.'

A censuring reflex *had* been there, for which the nun reproached herself.

'Do you want to tell me about them?'

His least attractive smirk appeared. A fabrication might be fun. Except his inventing a sexual theme was scarcely accidental. There were prurient elements to the nightmare—again insensible—made manifest by the clammy discharge he found sometimes on his sheets, unwholesome and incriminating.

'A little vicarious titillation, Ms. Zoë?'

This time the nun remained sedate. She let her neutral silence be his answer.

'No? Well, I'll spare you, then. The point is I can't sleep. You'd better give Quack Cahill a call and ask her to whip up another potion.'

'Has the nausea persisted, too?'

'That I can handle.'

'Perhaps we can decrease the dosage. I'll phone her today.'

'Fine. Now, about Ms. Dana and her mettlesome neurosis. The negativity she puts out is inhibiting my effectiveness as a teacher.'

130

'As I understand it, you made scant effort to help her feel welcome.'

'She wasn't welcome. Isn't. She's a nuisance—an ineffectual token to your vacuous conventions.'

'And you wonder at her hostility?'

'No, I wonder at your subjecting me—not to mention Marcy—to it.'

'Melanie.'

'Who?'

'We've discovered Marcy's real name is Melanie.'

'Oh?'

'I'm sure you've surmised by now that Marcy came to us as a bit of a mystery. I would appreciate it if you would begin to call her Melanie.'

'When did all this happen?'

'Will you?'

He checked his eagerness to garner the details.

'Sure—Marcy, Melanie—close enough. Who named her Marcy? You?'

'As a matter of fact, yes.'

'Pretty good guess. So, what about Ms. Dana?'

'I'll suggest she sit in the hall. You'll keep your door open, of course.'

'Of course.'

'Good. I'm told, by the way, you're quite a taskmaster.'

'She'll learn the game. Teaching her some memory

techniques will be the trick.'

'Weaned, I trust, of any amateur psychoanalysis on your part.'

Had Marcy/Melanie said something? Or had his own behavior raised suspicion? If the nun were totally convinced he was trespassing on her domain, he knew she would put a stop to it.

'Idle curiosity, Ms. Zoë, that's all, never fear. Your primacy as Chief Headshrinker isn't my concern.'

'Let us hope, for the sake of Melanie's continuing in your class, that this is true.'

He started to leave. She stopped him.

'Aren't you forgetting something?'

She pointed to his medicine.

'God forbid I leave without Communion.'

He kneeled before her desk as at an altar, palms together, lips apart.

'I am not amused, Mr. Papp.'

'Nevertheless.'

He shook three pills from the container (which he pocketed), popped them into his mouth, gulped, rose, and left.

She had been a trifle greedy, he reflected, pulling rank like that. But there was time. And losses in material could always be regained when, in development, one still had the edge.

* * *

How confession soothed the soul! How good it was to be forgiven! Sister Dana felt much better. An hour with Sister Zoë had helped to clarify a host of issues— "Marcy" being most notable among them. It had not been a confession in a formal way, of course, but the sense of expiation was the same. The elder nun had listened in that special mode she had, when the pretext was to "have a little chat". Her silences were understanding, and when she spoke her words were truly non-judgmental, helpful, caring. In this regard the chats were more restorative than was penance, where the repertoire was limited to prayer.

Then, too, some things had not required explaining. The tears that had trickled down the young nun's cheeks told all. Sister Zoë had sympathized. Love was not a state about which any human being need feel ashamed—even when it awakened sexuality. Bodies loved no less than spirits, hearts no less than minds. Many forms of loving sprang from each. People simply had to choose the forms best suited to their needs. Nuns were people. Their needs fostered choices, too. But nuns were also guided by the canons of their faith, which exacted from them certain sacrifices. It was of these that Sister Zoë at last had spoken. And Sister Dana, eager to atone, welcomed sound advice, adopting it to meet her current situation.

She had hated Julian, for instance. Even if she had Marcy's interests selfishly at heart, what she felt toward Julian was wrong. Which was not to say that he was any less guilty of harboring vile intentions. She was still convinced he did. But her indulging wicked thoughts was not the way to combat his. She saw that now. If Marcy were to be protected, she would have to alter her approach.

Except she had to sit in the hall, henceforward, during his class. When Sister had suggested this it came as a relief (all the further from Julian's animosity). In the light of her remodeled resolution, however, she had her doubts—though she certainly was within her rights to peek in occasionally, which might be better. Believing he was not being watched, Julian would be more likely to show his hand.

Yes, it would be better. And she would have the privacy to monitor her own emotions, reflecting on their genesis, weeding out impurities, bolstering fresh commitments to both Marcy and her Lord—to Melanie, rather. Melanie, Melanie, Melanie, Melanie. She had to stamp the change inside her head. Why was that so hard?

* * *

'Good afternoon, Julian.'

'Solved it, eh?'

She snapped her fingers. He smiled, then acknowledged her guardian.

'Sister Dana.'

'Mr. Papp. Have a good class, Melanie. I'll be outside in case you need me.'

Julian, with an effort, swallowed a snide retort. He had gotten the nun withdrawn to an acceptable position. Best leave well enough alone.

Teacher and student took their seats.

'So, we're both being "christened" today—to borrow a Zoëian term. You're Melanie now?'

'Uh huh.'

'Melanie what?'

'Don't start, Julian.'

'So M&M is still standing guard.'

'If you mean the Miniature Man, his name is Benjamin.'

'Well I'll be damned; identities are popping up all over. Has all this come to light apace with that fuzz atop your noggin?'

'You think it's ugly, don't you?'

'Cute as a bug's ear. Don't avoid my question.'

'I'm not here to answer your questions. Are you going to teach me this game or not?'

He spread his hands in a conciliatory gesture.

'Show me your solution.'

With an adeptness that he found amusing—for it was a parody of his own—Melanie set up the board. The mating moves were correct. He handed her a folded piece of paper, which she rightly assumed was her homework problem, indicating she put it away for later. The lesson then proceeded.

Meanwhile, Sister Dana wrestled with an elusive magnanimity. Julian's politeness helped—as did the talk she and Melanie had on the way to class, in which she had finally amassed sufficient courage to apologize for her behavior that night in the girl's room. She had not visited since, and was overwhelmed with gratitude when Melanie said she had missed her, even suggested that the visits might resume. After all the hideous mistakes she had made, it seemed a miracle that they were not being held against her. Melanie had hardly remembered—as opposed to having forgotten—had merely let the matter drop as if it were of little significance. A sense of reprieve gave new strength to the nun's determination to tread, with all concerned, on more hallowed ground.

What were they up to? She checked her watch. The hour was half over. For the last fifteen minutes she had heard nary a sound. Putting aside the book she brought, she walked the two steps to the door.

With her mouth stretched into a silly grin from her palms compressing her cheeks, Melanie sat, elbows on the table, scrutinizing the board. To everything outside the checkered plane, she was oblivious. Julian, on the other hand, was studying the girl—or so it appeared from the angle he held his head. He sat erect, expectant. Like a cat, she thought, a fierce white panther poised to spring on its unsuspecting prey. His stillness was uncanny, mesmerizing. An impulse to call out and warn her ward possessed the nun. And yet she was unable, as if the awful tension—and its fascination—held her in its enervating power.

Melanie moved a chess piece. Julian leaped.

'Marcy!'

Both players started at the cry. The nun stood red-faced in the doorway.

'I'm terribly sorry. Forgive me, please.'

Melanie looked at her inquiringly.

'I just peeked in this very minute to see, and… Well, I… Julian, I mean. He seemed to jump right out at you. I…'

'Oh, that. He always makes his moves that way. It's just a trick to keep whoever he's playing with off guard.'

Julian was annoyed by the interruption (as well as by his student's flip analysis of his technique).

'Is our time up, then?'

'No, I'm sorry, no… You have fifteen minutes left.'

Still confused, the nun did not withdraw. Julian grew impatient.

'Well?'

'Oh. Yes, I'm going. Forgive me… I'll be right outside. Sorry.'

She retreated to her chair out in the hall.

'I'm beginning to think that woman is a patient here, not a therapist.'

'Shhh. She's neither.'

'What is she, then?'

'Just a nun.'

'Just a nun? Just your normal Bible-toting paranoiac homosexual nun?'

'What?'

'Oh, come now. You're not that naïve.'

Melanie was angry with him instantly. She made her voice a hissing whisper.

'You just be quiet, Julian!'

'Not that there's anything wrong with being…'

'I mean it!'

He stopped. He waited for her to calm down. Her knuckles were white with the pressure in her fists. Seconds passed and still she clenched them tightly.

'Look at your hands, Melanie. Or should I call you Marcy?'

She looked. They seemed foreign. It took a monumental effort just to open them—which she made. She breathed in slowly, held it, then exhaled. With caution, Julian proceeded.

'Didn't you know, honestly?'

She found herself nodding in affirmation.

'Relax. It isn't your concern, it's hers.'

'But she's my closest friend.'

'And gay. So what?'

She turned away. Her thoughts and feelings were too entangled, too contradictory, too perplexing to have to cope with everything at once. The more she tried to sort things out, the more confused she grew. Her hands again crept into fists as tears welled into her eyes.

'Stop it!'

Immediately Sister Dana was at the door.

'Something wrong?'

Julian scowled at the intrusion. Melanie, responding once again to his severity, recovered.

'It's okay, Sister. He likes to yell at me whenever I do something stupid. He forgets that things he thinks are obvious maybe aren't so obvious to me.'

Melanie stood. Julian protested.

'Class isn't over.'

'What time is it, Sister?'

'Ten to three.'

'Close enough. See you Friday, Julian.'

He stayed seated.

'We'll pick up right where we left off, Melanie.'

She fixed him with an insolent look.

'I may not remember.'

She exited with Sister Dana.

'Don't worry, I'll remind you.'

* * *

Gotta have tits, Elmo, huge knockers. None of these flat-chested skateboard types.

Fuck off.

That one! That one!

I drive; I choose. And shut that fool thing off.

Don't shove that beaver-plucker in my face, fuckhead. God only knows where it's been.

Wouldn't you like to know?

Stan, you're sick, you know that?

Me? You should see ole Elmo here, bustin' bottoms with that pile driver of his. Get it? Pile driver?

There! Elmo, whataya want, man? Didya see the hair on that babe?

Fuck off.

What's that for?

The heat rub? Elmo smears it all over his rubber, man, before he butt-fucks 'em.

You're puttin' me on. Really, Elmo?

Yup.

You guys have really done this before?

Sure, Pauly, whataya think? We got two last month. Didn't we, Elmo?

Yup.

Elmo! There! Come on, man. Whatarya lookin' for?

A loner.

Shit, man, that'll take all night.

Fuck off.

There! There's one.

Where?

With the backpack, see? Slow up.

She's a baby, you guys.

Makes for a tighter fit, eh Elmo? Look at that mane!

Get ready, Stan.

Jesus, what are you gonna do with those?

Elmo, I think we got us a chicken-shit here. You gonna piss yerself, Pauly?

No. Just askin'.

Relax. We don't stick 'em 'til after. Crack the back door. And rip off some strips of that tape.

Now. Now!

Julian's eyes shot open. Like ink on felt, the outlines of

the dream began to blur. He scanned the fleeing company for clues as to who they were, not recognizing anyone, nor seeing himself among them. Unless these indistinguishable figures were aspects, alter egos? The very prospect caused his mind to cringe.

A van with a fisheye window distorting streets of glaring neon; voices; vulgar voices, in a choir of brute intent; this was all he could salvage; the rest had decomposed.

Julian tossed off the bedclothes. A nasty taste defiled his mouth. He walked to the bathroom, knelt before the toilet bowl, and vomited. It did not help.

Back in his room again, the air was dank, oppressive. He felt suffocated. He had to leave. He quickly dressed and went outdoors.

A gust of frigid predawn wind fixed him with a shock, then bore him up to the wooded hills, gratefully benumbed.

* * *

Now, well into her "schooling", Melanie, having been reintroduced to all her teachers, was settling into the new routine. Her classes were as varied as the personalities of those who taught them, ranging from the challenging intensity of Julian's, to the sweet nebulosity of Mr. Jimmy's. Theirs were her favorites, oddly. In between were Sister Dana's Bible Studies—simply a continuation of the evening readings (which, after being tacitly curtailed, had now resumed), Drawing with Sister Morgan—a birdlike nun with a passionate love of nature, Math from Mrs. Lowry—who really was a math teacher so she knew what she was doing (though she had a knack for making it uninteresting), Psychology from Sister Deborah—whose choosing to teach by lecture was unfortunate; she had a speech defect that made the most serious things she said sound funny, and finally English from Mrs. Soames—a stickler for proper grammar with a dogged faith in composition-writing as the key to mastering language. Few of the courses were likely to rate college accreditation, but they provided stimulus enough to keep the young girl's mind alert.

'That's the chess player, isn't it?'

'Uh huh.'

'Your drawing skills are very well developed, Melanie. This is excellent. Where did you learn?'

'Don't know.'

'May I see your other sketches?'

She handed over the pad she had been given the previous week.

'Sister Dana... Sister Zoë... The chess player again. What's his name?'

'Julian Papp.'

'Ah, yes. Here's another of him… And another. Mr. Papp seems to be a favorite subject.'

'He holds still a lot. It's easy to see him in my head.'

'All of these are from memory?'

'Uh huh.'

She turned another page. Julian's livid spectacles glared out from the paper, enlarged, distorted, the charcoal used to render them ground in savagely. Blind yet seeing, the dominating lenses seemed to emanate a miscreant emotion. They attacked and at the same time lured—a dramatic combination.

'This one's very different from the rest.'

The girl glanced up, noting the drawing to which the nun referred, then continued with her work.

'I was mad at him that day. He can be mean sometimes.'

'He looks positively ferocious here. What did he do to make you draw him like this?'

'He said something nasty about a friend of mine.'

'I'll have to watch my tongue.'

The next page was blank, though the shadow of another sketch showed through. Sister Morgan turned the page. The shadow darkened. Another turn revealed a strange looking man with exaggerated hands, and an even more extravagant right eye. He sat amid a fantastic assortment of stuff, holding what looked like a tiny wooden man.

'And this?'

Melanie looked.

'Benjamin.'

'I don't recognize the name. Or the face. Is he a patient?'

'No. He's somebody I know, or used to.'

Melanie suddenly remembered the drawings she had done at the back of the pad. She blushed. She did not want the nun to see them. Pretending to continue with her work, she listened while the pages rustled, hoping with all her might that the nun would stop before the last few were turned.

Finding a long succession of empty pages, Sister Morgan flipped the covers closed, replacing the pad at the foot of Melanie's chair.

'Have you shown your work to Sister Zoë?'

'I haven't shown anybody. Except you.'

'I think you should. You're very talented, Melanie.'

The nun watched as slender fingers guided the charcoal. They moved with a confidence unusual for a teenager. The rigidity, the awkward allegiance to representational form typical of adolescent art were nowhere evident. Melanie's images were bold and expressive, imbued with a candid energy that captured essences. Crude, of course. Naive. But tapping levels well beneath the superficial.

With a piece of chalk Melanie colored the pallor of Julian's face and hands.

'If you try to imagine your strokes beginning behind the form, then wrapping around out front, you'll enhance the sense of three dimensions.'

'Like this?'

'That's it. And don't forget that negative shapes create positive shapes outside of them. It's like that checkerboard you've sketched. Are those squares black on a field of white, or white on a field of black? Understand what I mean?'

'I think so. I sometimes look at Julian that way. Everything outside of him has shape and color, and he's just this blank white space.'

'Judging from your work, it seems you feel a lot of things about Julian. That one you have there is very sympathetic.'

Melanie considered the pasty flesh, the masked eyes looking out through lines and smudges. She had made him sad this time.

'He can be nice, too. I think I draw him so much because I'm trying to figure him out. Mostly I feel sorry for him.'

'Because he looks so odd?'

'No. Because he's so lonely.'

* * *

Julian considered the snowflake in his hand. It had not melted on contact, for his flesh was freezing cold. But as he brought it nearer to his face his breath transformed the fragile crystal into dew. If frozen again, would it fashion yet another novel symmetry… as did The Game… the hundreds of games, the thousands—from a distance all just Chess—yet, when looked at closely, each variation as wondrously unique as any snowflake: as intricate, as beautiful, as infinite?

He watched as the flurries danced against a brooding backdrop, each nonconforming particle exultant in the wind's caprice, until gravity carried out its sentence and committed each to an earthbound anonymity.

The fallen gathered. Already blades of grass were bowed, weeds and bushes coated, twigs and tree limbs dressed in hoary sleeves.

White on white, Julian's immobile form became invisible.

Finally he stirred. Which way? Did it matter? Seizures, nightmares, nausea, and pills conspired to overcast Julian's mind with the same gunmetal gray that bruised the sky. There was no refuge. Nor was there the exhilaration of being caught up in lines of play. He heard the wind. He saw the drifts piling up at random.

Order. Order was a ruse in Nature. How could there be order when so much was left to chance? Whereas in Chess there was no element of chance. Reason, logic, calculation—these a mind could master. What was "mere chance", compared to the Royal Game?

He slipped and fell.

The chapel bell rang out. He counted eight dull distant throbs before it halted. He did not rise. Instead he lay on his back with his wrists crossed over his breast like a cadaver, letting the snow collect—along with his suicidal thoughts.

Humiliation; that was part of it. But losing. That was...

A crow cawed sharply.

Julian flinched, then watched it swoop and come to rest in a nearby tree.

'Black devil.'

It cawed again as if annoyed at Julian's presence.

'Stupid beast.'

It cawed a third time.

'Shit. Goddamnit; can't I even freeze to death in peace?'

He lumbered to his feet and chased the bird away with a near-miss snowball.

'Nuns and crows must have a common ancestor.'

He had to laugh. He felt a little better.

Perhaps he would pay Ms. Zoë an unexpected visit.

* * *

By the time he arrived, the smile he had donned was frozen on his face (a rigid tabloid of his impetus for coming).

'Gracious, Mr. Papp, you're blue!'

'An aesthetically pleasing shade?'

'You'll catch your death, going out-of-doors in those summer clothes.'

'I nearly did.'

'What?'

'I threw a snowball at it, and it flew away.'

'Now you're being facetious. Here.'

She took him by the arm and led him over to the radiator.

'Stand right there while I get you a blanket.'

He worked his jaw, restoring some sensation to his lips. The chill had made his diction feel retarded. Sister Zoë returned.

'How long had you been out in that freezing cold?'

He did not know or care. She wrapped the blanket around his shoulders.

'Not all night, I hope! Don't you have a winter coat?'

He shook his head. The heat was slowly penetrating— as was the warmth of the nun's concern. The Game perhaps could wait while he thawed out.

'I'll have your mother bring one when she visits.'

'My mother! I thought we agreed she wouldn't come unless I gave permission.'

'I'm afraid she has insisted.'

'*She's* insisted? Who's in charge here?'

'It's true, I could have overruled. You are of age and in our care. But frankly, Mr. Papp, I feel this moratorium you've imposed is somewhat cruel. Your mother, presently, needs some reassurance. Why deny it to her?'

He paused to weigh the advantages, and especially the disadvantages, of his mother's incarnation as the Black King's Queen. For instance, she might pose a threat to his continuing with The Game. It was she, after all, who had chosen St. Francis. It was she who paid the fees. So it was she who could determine if her son would stay or leave—thus underscoring another liability of Julian's eccentricities.

He had always refused to play for money. He had also refused to do anything but play. Therefore, he was financially dependent on his mother, who had, in this, indulged him absolutely.

'How much contact have you had with Mother Dear?'

'She telephones.'

'Often?'

'Yes.'

'Daily?'

'Not quite.'

'And what's your diagnosis?'

'That would be presumptuous.'

'You contradict yourself, Ms. Zoë. You've deigned to act "therapeutically" where she's concerned; you must have come to certain conclusions about her mental health—or lack thereof.'

'Julian, your mother…'

His scowl reminded her of his insistence on "Mr. Papp."

'Oh, stop that! We know each other well enough to drop the formalities, don't you think?'

'No, I don't. I know almost nothing about you.'

'Only because you haven't asked.'

'And regardless of all your copious notes, I doubt that your idea of me is all that comprehensive. Especially if you've been listening to my mother.'

'Admittedly, you remain something of an enigma.'

'So?'

'So it is high time that you let down your defenses, opened up a dialogue that's sincere. Your mother wants to take you home. I wasn't able to convince her that you weren't ready. I'm not sure I'm convinced of that myself. How do you feel, really feel?'

'It's too soon.'

'Which means you're still disturbed about some things. What things, Julian?'

He might well have asked himself what a longer stay would accomplish. What was he doing there? Why did the thought of leaving stir a minatory dread? But he did not ask. Instead he gave priority to The Game.

The nun somewhat softened her tone.

'Tell me about "the meadow".'

He tensed. He must be cautious here. Once before he had tried to articulate that all-pervasive consciousness. He had been misunderstood—disastrously—his metaphors dissected with a clinical precision that undermined his faith in what they pictured.

'Timelessness. It's more than that, but I know my meadow is outside time.'

'Why is that important?'

'If you played tournament chess you'd know. The time clock is a player's most relentless enemy—or ally, if he knows a way to nullify its power. I knew how. While my opponents were sweating out the minute hand, I was somewhere else.'

'Can you describe it?'

'No.'

'Yet you call it a "meadow".'

'A meadow in the sense that it represents a kind of clearing.'

He studied her reactions carefully before continuing.

'If somehow you were able to peel away your outer skin and feel things as your body did the moment it was born, that would give you some idea of the sensitivities there. A breath becomes a breeze. The air has texture. Thoughts are passed by touches, not through words.'

'It isn't a lonely place, then?'

'No. No, it's the only un-lonely place I've ever known. Someone is there, a presence unlike my own… feminine, but kindred. It/she gives me something I can't explain, something I carry with me when I go back to the game. A kind of clarity.'

'But this place, in itself, has nothing to do with chess?'

'Nothing. Except whatever it is finds chess a sympathetic medium. But no, it isn't chess. It's even beyond winning.'

'Winning isn't the most important thing to you?'

'It's not an issue; I never lose. Not when I'm in touch.'

'And if you did?'

'I don't.'

There was a pause. Much of what he revealed had not occurred to him before.

'Thank you, Julian.'

'For what?'

'For trusting me. For helping me to understand. I won't pretend I do yet, not fully, but you've given me at least a sense of the loss you feel you've suffered. Haven't you experienced even a glimpse since the onset of the seizures?'

'No. From aura, to fit, to nightmare; that's been the progression. What do you suppose is next; insanity?'

'I doubt that. Not if we can talk about it, try to think it through.'

'And what about my mother?'

'I'll ask her to delay.'

He was satisfied. Chances still looked good for White. In his mind, the shadow of his hand reached toward the board.

* * *

The mouth was wrong. The nose was a bit too big. She had even misplaced the two tiny moles. But the resemblance, for Melanie's purpose, was accurate enough. With the charcoal's edge, she began the kinky swirls, a wonderfully thick corona this time. If it would only grow as fast as she could draw it! The face took on a whole new character as its outlines were adorned. She let the ringlets run right off the page. A mane! With flowers! She crushed in petals with her chalk.

She held the pad toward the mirror, her face beside it, comparing. The reversed image tended to accentuate the drawing's flaws, but not her own. Her three-dimensional features were unquestionably prettier. And when her crown of stubbly hair matured, she knew she would be beautiful. Would it come in straight or wavy, in graceful strands or undulating curls? She had tried out possibilities on paper, reserving the latter pages of her sketchbook to that end. It was Sister Morgan's nearly finding these the day before that had caused the girl such heart-pounding alarm. Maybe they were vain, but doing them gave Melanie a special pleasure.

Rather than risk their discovery again, she carefully detached all six self-portraits from the pad, and laid them out across her bed to see which one she liked best.

There was a knock at the door.

She hastily gathered them up.

'Just a minute.'

She hid them in her dresser drawer, face down beneath her panties, then grabbed the pad and flipped back through its pages.

'Come in.'

As she began reworking the sketch she had done the previous day in class, Sister Dana entered with a package.

'Don't tell me you're actually working on something besides those silly chess problems.'

Melanie closed the sketchbook altogether, hoping to avoid a similar comment on her drawing's subject matter. She did spend inordinate amounts of time on solving Julian's riddles. Novice though she was, the poeticism he had ascribed to certain attributes of the game had made a strong impression. An affinity was there, as was a desire to please her teacher—please, impress, or show him up, in accordance with her ever-changing moods.

He did not coddle her. She respected that.

The latest problem, for example, was even harder than the first—a real mind-tickler—and had consumed many hours of trial and error already. But, oddly, she was not discouraged. Something in the nature of these challenges enticed her.

The package caught her eye.

'What's that?'

'A present.'

'For me?'

The Sister nodded, pleased at having aroused some curiosity.

'Can I open…'

'May I…'

'May I open it?'

'Not with those hands!'

Her hands were absolutely black with charcoal, as was the streak, from a well-scratched itch, along her nose. Melanie excused herself to wash.

The nun glanced down at the abandoned sketchbook. A fleeting sense of tact repressed her impulse to peruse it. The book somehow looked personal—thus all the more alluring. She heard a water-tinkling sound beyond the bathroom door.

The temptation was irresistible. With affected nonchalance, she flicked open the cover, revealing a smudgy image of... herself. Multiple emotions stirred: gladness at the sentiment, guilt at having peeked, fear lest she be caught, and then, on looking closer, a stinging indignation, for Sister Dana thought the portrait was brazenly unflattering. To her, the soot-filled eyes betrayed licentiousness, the mouth was unmistakably embittered, and the chin receded with nothing shy of truculence. She clapped the cover closed. So that was how she was viewed! Her fingers tightened on the package as Melanie returned.

'Now may I?'

She displayed her hands for inspection.

The nun's resentment softened.

'Please?'

'You may.'

In two quick rips the wrapping fell away, disclosing Sister Dana's precious Bible.

'But this is yours, Sister.'

'I want you to have it.'

'But your father gave it to you the day you became a nun. You told me so. No, I couldn't.'

Melanie was genuinely moved. Commensurately, Sister Dana's pique dissolved.

'Please. Were he alive I know he wouldn't mind. I've written you a dedication just inside the cover.'

Melanie found it.

My Angel,

Though thou may never fully know thy preciousness to me, if Jesus loves His children half as much as I love thee, we will meet in Heaven,

Forever,
Dana

Watching Melanie read her heartfelt inscription, the nun relived the moments of its writing. She had been alone, locked inside her room, curtains drawn, lampshades taken from the bulbs to intensify the light. She had faced the mirror naked, gazing at the spectacle of a sinner. At her feet had lain her Bible opened to the lines her father's prideful hand had penned. Beneath these she had scrawled her own to Melanie. In her fist was her father's razor.

It had been the night the girl had briefly disappeared, the night the nun had almost lost her mind, and worse, her soul. Had her thoughts been less distraught, she would have recognized that the act she had stood contemplating would have damned her, *for eternity*, to Hell. And yet her hand had nearly carried out the fatal deed, was poised, in fact, above the vein, when a voice called out from deep inside the mirror. "Ring the bell," it said, "the bell." She had stopped... her body trembling, her wits straining to decipher the phrase's meaning—then it dawned; the girl was merely lost, not run away!

'Sister?'

Melanie recalled her to the present.

'Yes, my sweet?'

'You're not going away, are you?'

She smiled.

'No, love… No.'

'I'm glad.'

She reached up and laid her palm on the young nun's cheek.

'Thank you, Sister. I'll treasure it. Always.'

The nun was overwhelmed by this unprecedented gesture (never before had the girl initiated contact). She stammered a confused goodbye, and, rejoicing inwardly, withdrew.

Melanie returned to the inscription. Above the one to her was its predecessor (in paler, faded ink):

My Angel,

It seems this day is one that I have longed for all my life. And now that it has come, I trust our Lord will smile unendingly, knowing He has conceived through such a humble man as me, a daughter such as you.

Your loving father

Melanie read the last three words again… then again. She sat there for a long while, softly sobbing.

***

'It is pwobable that dweams awe mewely chemical dischawges in the bwain, set off at wandom by wesidual mental enewgy accumulated duwing wakeful houws. Theiw subjective chawactew is due to the individual means by which infowmation emewges when conscious systems of pwocessing and owganization awe functionally opewative. Put mowe simply, the contingencies of sleep pweclude the mind's ability to awange its impwessions into compwehensible fowm.'

From the expression on Melanie's face, this "simplification" was no more intelligible than the sentences preceding it. But insofar as Sister Deborah seldom looked at her pupil's face, the girl's apparent perplexity went unnoticed.

'Now, with the advent of Sigmund Fweud, attempts wewe made to examine dweams symbolically. It was believed that theiw manifestations wepwesented those pewsonality twaits that the conscious mind wepwessed. Elabowate classification systems wewe designed to demonswate the welationship between specific psychological disowdews and wecuwwent dweam images. This focus on the "stuff of dweams" is, today, a pwinciple gwounds fow dismissing much of Fweud's wowk. Had he concent*w*ated on the ways a d*w*eame*w* desc*w*ibes unconscious expe*w*iences, his c*w*edibility might be yet intact. In othe*w* wo*w*ds, it is not what we d*w*eam that is symptomatic, it is how we choose to *w*elate it.'

There was a pause that lasted long enough for Melanie to grow self-conscious. Her doodling was arrested.

'Any questions so fa*w*?'

She smiled politely, shaking her head no. What if the Bishop moved to h6? She had not tried that yet. Or had she? The sketched-in chessboard above her notes was so crisscrossed with lines, the original position was illegible.

'… example to illust*w*ate this concept. Suppose a subject we*w*e to have a nightma*w*e about falling. Now falling is a common phobia that f*w*equently appea*w*s at both conscious and unconscious levels. Its occu*ww*ing in one's sleep, howeve*w*, does not necessa*w*ily mean that…'

Melanie shut out the lecture. Julian's class was tomorrow. She just *had* to have the problem solved by then. It would be tedious to draw the squares again, shading every other one. She looked away from the scribbly grid, trying to visualize a clear one in her head. She had to close her eyes. Slowly the board appeared. One by one, she set the pieces. Then she tried the Bishop move, examining as best she could its consequences. So far, so good; it forced the play. And the next two moves were obvious!

She opened her eyes to check on the nun. Her lips were still moving, face averted, pacing as usual back and forth, her fingers interlaced. Now what was she talking about? Dreams? The lecture brought to mind her talks with Benjamin. Was he a dream? He seemed too real. Sister Deborah apparently believed that dreams were nothing in themselves (or so Melanie gathered from the little she had understood). But if that were true, how could she explain Julian's arrival having been foreseen by the Miniature Man? He had known—just as he had known other things before they actually happened—or appeared to know. If dreams were only real inside the dreamer, that meant she herself had invented everything—Benjamin, his workshop, and every word he spoke, which somehow sounded not exactly right. Maybe she had only exaggerated things, made some rash assumptions or leaped to the wrong conclusions. The original carving, for instance— the ivory one... Maybe it reminded her of Julian but was not really him. But that also sounded less than accurate.

She let the Sister's voice back into her ears.

'So when, in the couwse of descwibing his expewiences, the subject shows some anxious sign, it is weasonable to assume the feaw of falling is a twait with which his consciousness contends.'

She stopped, lowered her prayer-poised hands from her chin, and looked to Melanie for comment.

'Cleaw?'

'I think so. But I disagree.'

'You disagwee? Don't be widiculous; it is not a question

of disagweeing. All you awe wequiwed to do is listen and compwehend.'

'But I've had dreams that weren't all make-believe.'

'Nonsense.'

'No, really. In one of them a man named Benjamin told me about my future. Then, in real life, it happened.'

'Just a coincidence, I'm suwe.'

The nun's dogmatic attitude raised Melanie's ire.

'And he knows things, too—things I know I couldn't know myself.'

'Most likely they awe things that you've fowgotten.'

This made Melanie angrier still. How dare the nun doubt Benjamin's existence? She lost her temper.

'What makes you so sure about your stupid theory!'

'Melanie!'

'I remember Benjamin! He's a dream but he's my friend, too!'

'Melanie, calm down.'

'I won't! You're a liar! Benjamin is real and he takes care of me and you're a liar!'

'Melanie, please!'

The insects screamed so loudly they sent shooting pains throughout her skull. The room and Sister Deborah disappeared. Instead there was an open plot of ground, dry, hot, and cracked like sun-parched lips. An ant crawled past. It had a bit of food that it was dragging toward the shade. Another ant appeared. It looked like it was going to help. But no. It tried to steal the food. Another ant arrived, then came a third, each pinching meanly at the prize. The first ant fought them off. Their tactics changed. By turns the thieves began to bite and slash the owner's body. When it was maimed sufficiently, all three attacked at once. The food was snatched. The culprits fled. Their victim lay dismembered in the dirt.

'Sis*tews*! She's in he*we*!'

The scene disbanded in a swarm of incandescent spots, then, cooling, re-congealed. Black on white, nuns against the stuccoed walls, faces fixed, habits posed in a rigid choreography, while Melanie shrank… smaller… smaller… to diminutive proportions, cowering in a square of light on the fringes of a starkly checkered plane.

'Melanie?'

The checkered landscape altered, warped, and, like a dividing cell, split in two. A hand advanced, white and bloodless.

'Melanie!'

'Sister Zoë?'

'What is all this?'

The girl had retreated to a corner of Sister Deborah's room—which at the moment was absurdly overcrowded.

'She's all *w*ight, eve*wy*body. Thank you. We'll handle it f*w*om he*we*. Thank you.'

Those whom the nun's alarm had summoned were ushered from the tiny room. Sister Zoë remained. She sat down on the floor beside her patient.

'Can you tell me what happened?'

The images retreated to the dark from whence they had come. Melanie looked to Sister Deborah for aid.

'We we*w*e talking about d*w*eams, *w*emembe*w*?'

No, she did not. But she must; she knew she must. A memory was stalking her. She felt its presence looming in the shadows of her mind, spoiling for its chance to overtake her. Something "bad".

That was it. And they all knew, and nobody would tell her what it was.

'Tell me, please, I have to know. I can't remember on my own. You have to help me, Sister. Sister, please?'

'I told you, we we*w*e discussing…'

'Excuse me, Sister Deborah. I think I'd like a moment here with Melanie alone. Would you mind?'

With a slightly forced humility, the nun complied.

Sister Zoë had understood what Melanie was asking. She turned back solemnly to the frightened girl, resolving that the time, at last, had come.

'Melanie. The truth is, you were raped. The authorities don't know by whom. You were found out in the desert, bound and gagged and beaten and left for dead.'

The words at first were merely that—words—vague abstractions, conveying an idea only, with none of its reality. "Raped"? What did it mean? Of course it had horrific connotations. But that was reputation, rumor, drummed-in fear to keep potential targets on their guards. What, though, did it mean in her own experience? Or, should she ask, what had it meant?

The gap between the words and what they represented narrowed. Meaning, joined by memory, crowded in. And the dreaded insect sounds, more fiercely than ever, resumed their screeching.

* * *

Sister Zoë put the latest entry on Melanie's condition into the manila folder and pushed closed the cabinet drawer, which made a doleful "clunk". Not much to write. Melanie had relapsed. Little more to add. The scream she had screamed struck reverberating chords of doubt in Sister Zoë's mind. All her patience, all her care in helping the girl rebuild a lost identity seemed swept away—a sandcastle smoothed by one resurgent wave. Professionally, she had made a mistake. It happened—had and would, and though never pleasant, mistakes were useful ways by which to learn.

But failure, in this instance, could be charged to an intuitive error, and this was why the nun was so aggrieved. Instinct was what had prompted her to make the revelation. The time, she felt, had been right. Yet look at the result. Her patient had drifted back into that no-man's-land from whence she had come—eyes glazed over, attention gone, functioning somnambulistically. The regression distressed her deeply. Had she only waited. Had she only realized that the truth was still too fresh a wound for Melanie to acknowledge.

She shook herself. The deed was done. Regretting it would not erase the blame. Perhaps the girl had already improved. She got her coat and scarf, and, bundling up, went out on her morning rounds.

* * *

What Sister Zoë perceived with guilty sorrow, Sister Dana viewed with guilty happiness. Her putting Melanie to bed the night before had stirred a sweet nostalgia. And beyond the caring, the touching, the coddling intimacy un-rebuffed, the nun again experienced the joy of being needed. That was what she had really missed—Melanie's dependence on her… Marcy's, rather. For in her heart she found herself returning to the former name. It was Marcy she had known and loved, still loved, in fact. Melanie was much too independent, strong-willed, too complex. Her needs had long outrun the nun's ability to fulfill them. Marcy's needs were simpler. How easy it would be to slip back into all her fond routines, with Marcy.

But the young nun realized that this would not do. Her former love had been impure. She must not let her baser self regain its domination. So Melanie was whom she must address—Melanie. She must look upon this relapse as a God-sent second chance. It would not last, but while it did, she knew the Lord was watching. Could her love be fashioned into a form acceptable to Him, or would it once again revert to profanation? Judgment (and temptation) lay in wait.

The girl was up, sitting in her robe and slippers, staring out the window. The veil had not yet lifted. Sister Dana made the bed. The pillow was still warm. A tiny hair lay atop its cover—Melanie's hair—another sure reminder.

A soft knock signaled Sister Zoë's arrival.

'Good morning, Sister.'

'Good morning, Sister Dana. Any change?'

She cast a glance at the silent girl and shook her head.

The elder nun approached.

'Melanie?'

She stooped beside her patient, studying the distant look now governing her gaze.

'Good morning, Melanie. Did you have a restful sleep?'

She did not answer. She did not hear.

A mouse had captured her attention as it scurried along a dusty shelf, looking frantically among the books for a place to hide. It halted, its polished eyes alert, trained on its pursuer—who took a step. The mouse darted off, then disappeared.

'Did she, Sister Dana?'
'She got up once to use the bathroom. That was all.'

The tracks went in; none came out. The space was very dark. Melanie gingerly removed a volume. It was very heavy; it took two hands. The mouse was there, trembling in the corner. She tugged out another book to admit more light. The chase, again, was on.

'Does she hear us, I wonder?'
'Sometimes, I think. She'll do things if you ask her: brush her teeth, wash her face, put on or take off her clothes.'

The mouse found shelter wedged behind a range of jagged mountains in a moonlit world she had not seen before. Was Benjamin at work on something new? He had not told her. Forgetting the mouse, she attended to the unfamiliar scene.

'Has she spoken?'
'She moves her lips at times as if she's speaking, but never makes a sound.'

The cubicle was studded with varieties of cacti, in a landscape marked by brittle rock and eerie dried-up creeks. Beneath a tree, a green-skinned tree with spike-like thorns in place of leaves, a toy-sized van was parked, headlights beaming across the sage. The van looked black, had racing stripes, spoked oversized wheels, and a convex porthole that glowered like some iridescent eye. The doors in back, she noticed, were ajar. She poked them open with her finger and stole a peek inside. A roof light lit incredible detail: dashboard ornaments, high-tech gadgetry, speakers, tape deck, bucket seats, then odds and ends strewn about on a plushly carpeted floor. She saw scissors, tape, a high school backpack, a jar of Vaseline, a tube of heat rub, cigarettes, matches, beer cans, a heap of shredded clothing, random clumps of matted hair, and, in the middle of it all, a brownish stain, the sight of which provoked a twinge of nausea.

'Melanie? I have to go now. Sister Dana will stay with you. I'll come back to visit later.'

She stroked the fuzzy head then motioned Sister Dana to the door.

What was missing? The driver? Was that what Benjamin had left out? Maybe there had been an accident. Apprehensive now, she strained to see beyond the van, but was too short. She gathered some books from the shelves and stacked them in a pile on which to stand.

'If there is any change, I want to know immediately.'
'Yes, Sister.'

Three men were now in view. Two were posed in active postures (climbing down a wash). The lighting made their faces look grotesque. A third (ahead of them in shadow) was perched above a spot discoloring the ground. The more Melanie stared, the more disturbing grew the situation—and yet she could not tear her eyes away. Something bad was happening. Those faces—the lights—the sickening smell of alcohol—the taste of dirt and blood and fear—the pain! The pain was everywhere! And then that awful, awful shrieking noise that…

His hands upon her shoulders stopped the insect sounds completely. Benjamin turned her wincing face aside.

And what do you think you're up to, eh? Snooping?

I was just…

Snooping. Out of bounds.

But Benjamin…

There will be no buts.

But...

What did I say?

She stuck out her lower lip reprovingly. He hoisted her up by her doll-like arms and carried her away. Over her shoulder she watched the headlights fade into the dusky gloom, then finally disappear.

She tickled his nose with a lock of her hair as he walked.

I'll sneeze you to smithereens.

Where's that?

Just North of Kingdom Come.

She was happy he was not really mad. He was never really mad, ever. Besides, if there were something he did not want her to see, he should have hidden it better.

She remembered the mouse.

I saw a mouse.

The one in tennis shoes, or the bowler hat?

I think he had on tennis shoes.

That would be Mort. Runs like the wind?

He was pretty fast.

That's Mort.

They were back in the main work area, where Benjamin set her down.

He led me to that desert.

Who?

Mort.

I'll have to have a talk with that rodent.

Isn't it ready?

It is. You aren't. The fools.

Fools?

The penguin brigade. Ah well, it's been pleasant having you for such a nice long visit—though it's time you got yourself back.

When do I get to see the...

Next time, maybe. Whenever you want to.

She was about to insist that he let her see now, but something held her back. She had seen enough, and did not like it, and wondered why the Miniature Man had made such ugly things… but when she turned to ask him, he was gone.

'Sister Dana?'

'Melanie!'

'How long have you been here?'

'Are you all right? Don't you remember? Are you really feeling better?'

She felt fine—though obviously there must have been something wrong if saying so caused surprise. She thought a moment.

'Oh! Sister Deborah.'

'You do remember.'

'Is she angry?'

'No. I don't think angry, just very concerned. We've all been very concerned.'

She felt a rush of foreboding.

'What day is it?'

'Friday.'

'The date, I mean.'

'Oh. Oh no, don't look so worried. It happened just last evening.'

She was relieved. This was unlike the times before,

then. Granted she had been away and could not account for much since attending Sister Deborah's class, but that terrible hollow feeling she recalled from lapses past had, thankfully, not recurred. And she did remember Benjamin, and the mouse. She must write everything down at once. She looked at the clock.

'Oh no. I've missed English and Math already!'

'Calm down. Sister cancelled all your classes. Your teachers have been notified.'

'What about Julian?'

'I'm sure Sister told him, too.'

The problem! She still had not solved it. How long did she have; three hours? She hastened to the chessboard.

'You're not thinking of going to Chess today, I hope.'

The Bishop. The Bishop? The Bishop! She tried the move, quickly testing it for flaws. It worked! It was beautiful, pure poetry, just like Julian said.

'Well, are you?'

She turned.

'I am now. Let's go have lunch. I'm starving.'

'First, I must tell Sister. You go ahead and get dressed.'

'And then what?'

'Wait for me.'

'Why can't I meet you in the cafeteria?'

'Because you're not supposed to be alone.'

'But Sister, I'm okay.'

'Just wait. I won't be long.'

The nun hurried out. Melanie got dressed.

* * *

Friday, November 7th, at 11:08 in the A.M. Sister Dana just left. I think she spent the night in the chair beside my bed. I'm not sure, though. Things haven't been too clear lately (sixteen hours I guess it's been), like lots of different movies squashed together. The last one is the clearest. I was a little girl again, visiting Benjamin. I was having fun. Except I saw something I wasn't supposed to. I don't know what that was now. Ants? I do remember watching these big red ants, and seeing a spot on the ground. No, on a carpet, in a van. That was it. The spot was on the floor of this van that had all sorts of stuff lying around inside. Outside, it was night. But I could see things, even in the dark. Faces, tiny faces like the ones on Julian's chessmen. Only these were ugly, bad faces. They scared me, but then Benjamin came and I wasn't frightened anymore. He took me away. I can go back, though, whenever I want. Benjamin said so.

Before that, I don't remember much, except that what started everything off was dreams. Sister Deborah said that they were nonsense. I said they weren't. That started an argument and I got mad and bam!

So now I'm going to go have lunch with Sister Dana, and after, go to Chess. I'm excited because this time I figured out the moves all by myself.

* * *

The cancellation of Melanie's class struck Julian as a rather curious move. It accomplished little, other than inciting him to ask a rash of questions—all of which "Ms." Zoë adroitly parried. "A minor setback," "probably nothing serious; just needs a bit of rest to set things right." Contending with such platitudes had been worse than swallowing his pills (although he had not swallowed his pills the entire day). Exactly what had happened? Why? How would it affect The Game? The girl would be well guarded; chances would be slim for a direct line of play— so better, temporarily, to shift his attack.

The snow was brittle underfoot. It packed with squeaky crunches. Stiff wind, bright sun, the sky a brilliant arctic blue. Stubborn scraps of rusty leaves still clung among the treetops. The air felt dry. It inundated the lungs with frigid shocks, purgative and invigorating. Julian's pace was brisk, and had carried him much farther than he had ever hiked before. New territory. After so much institutional monotony, this change of scene was blissful. No walls, no corridors, no antiseptic smells, no schedules, no clocks, no female supervision.

The nuns were like a platoon of mothers. Their vigilance was getting on his nerves. They watched, took notes, and submitted reports, until he felt his every act was being surreptitiously transcribed. Yet home, he knew, would be far worse. There the onus of his humiliation hovered like a thunderhead: the chess club. He had not returned. Nor would he.

A gust of wind made the branches chatter.

Forfeit. A forfeiture was a defeat. His first and last, that much he had determined. So why had he allowed himself to undertake another game, flirt with the narcotic of his black-and-white addiction? To and fro, back and forth, attack defend, advance retreat; an intercourse of mind that left the victor's ego satiated, the vanquished foe's destroyed. Ego was the habit-former. How easy it had been to feign transcendence—having never lost.

The snow was shallow. He changed direction, heading toward a rock-encrusted ridge.

Defeat was new, repugnant, even if he had never been outplayed. No, he had never been outplayed. In fact, the last match had been his, not lost or drawn—a clear-cut win. Perhaps his reputation, in his absence, had survived. The thought was like a splint to a broken wing. Except the seizure had made him look ridiculous—lying prostrate, limbs askew, eyelids fluttering like a pair of spring-snapped window shades.

A bizarre appearance was one thing; he had cultivated that. Being a laughingstock was quite another matter. No, he was not willing to go back there, even if his gift were to return.

His gift. Of what had *it* consisted? Vanity? Winning? Had he deceived the nun, deceived himself? Was crushing each opponent not the fundamental reason for his play?

Exertion from the climb made Julian sweat, his glasses fogging up with steam. He dared not take them off, for sun on snow, even filtered, caused him pain. Instead he groped on, nearly blind, until he felt himself descending, sharply.

The wind had stopped. He stopped, too. His lenses slowly cleared. Below him, in a spruce-lined glen, a weathered shack was nestled. Abandoned, surely. And yet, from where he stood, the windows looked intact. No road. Unless he had walked in circles, there could not be a road for miles. He scrambled down the leeward ridge. A makeshift slough defined a frozen spring. With a cautiousness that bordered on absurdity, he approached the cabin. The roof seemed sound. Its edges gleamed with jagged rows of icicles. A woodpile wore its wintry coat unruffled. There was an outhouse down a path whose boundaries showed as stiff, protruding weeds. He stepped up to the door—he knocked... turned the knob—it opened.

The shack was but a single room, though it seemed larger than it looked from outside. The hearth took up one corner, its stones and mortar charred. A wrought-iron spit above the grate was rigged to be turned by a crank. From rusting nails in a mesquite mantle, pots and kettles were hung. The bed consisted of blankets laid on a crib of pine needles. By the window stood a table and a pair of tree-stump chairs. A plate, a cup, and some silverware were waiting. An open cupboard dominated the northern wall—stocked with canned goods, mostly. Bags of rice and flour, dishes. There were no decorations, no knickknacks, photographs, or paintings. There was no clock. An hourglass by the fireplace was the only concession to time.

He went out to fetch some wood.

Clouds were forming to the west. They were low, displaying a snowstorm-laden gray, which soon might threaten flurries. Intending to retrace his footprints, Julian was concerned. But the cabin's welcome promised such a cozy warmth, he decided it was worth the risk. Maybe there was coffee. He could melt some snow and brew a pot, drink it, then be on his way. He dug down into the stack of logs to find some drier pieces, and, gathering an armload, went back inside.

He checked the shelves for matches. He found candles, lamp oil, a meerschaum pipe, a row of paperback books. He found a wooden chess set, too, in a checkered box that doubled as the board. He put it on the table, then proceeded with his search. In a box of kindling beside the hearth he found what he was after.

The pinesap sizzled, giving off an incense-like aroma that mingled with the smell of brewing coffee. He had found two canisters, each half full, alongside several others stocked with tea. From a rack of mugs he chose one with a sculpted female face, its handle formed by a looping braid of hair. With this, the chess set, and a blanket from the bed, he settled himself in front of the crackling fire.

* * *

'He doesn't answer. I don't think he's here.'

The nun came up behind her.

'Maybe when he heard your class was cancelled he made other plans.'

'Didn't you tell him I was coming?'

'No; you didn't ask me to.'

Exasperated, Melanie banged again. That she had solved the problem and now could not boast about her triumph was infuriating. Where could he have gone? She kicked the door.

'Melanie! That's enough. He obviously isn't in. Come on.'

'Wait. I want to leave a note. Let me borrow your pen. And a sheet of paper?'

Given them, she jotted down the three successive moves with Black's replies. She secured the note between the door and molding.

'There.'

'What's it supposed to mean?'

'He'll know.'

* * *

Gaunter versions of the chessmen stretched across the fire-lit board. Their flickering shadows seemed to cast a paralytic spell. Julian sat before them like a sphinx. He had taken off his glasses and, through irises flaming pink, the firelight lent his eyes a supernatural glow. They beamed a concentration laser-like with intensity, illuminating the ranks of occupied squares.

It came in a sudden flash of insight. Precipitate an exchange! Knight for Knight, night for nightmare— Ms. Zoë's account of Melanie's relapse in return for his description of his dream. The images that cursed his sleep came back to mind begrudgingly. Not all. Not most. But just those few which, by force of will, he had managed to retrieve, enough for him to trace them to their source—which had to be the file. Julian had suddenly come to a conclusion. The nightmare he had been having was a variation on a theme, the theme derived from Melanie's case history. Of course what his subconscious had projected was pure fiction, his imagination running wild with a few suggestive facts. But if these dark extrapolations held at least a grain of truth, perhaps they could be offered up in trade.

Yet what had he to offer, really? A smattering of reconstructed parts, a general outline? Like sorting through the pieces of a jigsaw puzzle, all he could isolate were the edges of its frame. And even these fit imperfectly.

Nonetheless, the move was right; that was absolutely clear.

The fire exploded with a snap. He stirred. Flames flicked out through the cremated logs like tongues from red-orange grins. The room was nearly dark. Hurriedly he put the set away. Was it night already? Frosted windows cloaked the hour of day. He wiped one with his sleeve. Outside it was snowing. Hard.

* * *

Her note was still there. After searching all the likely places, Melanie had circled back to see if he had returned. She banged again on the door as if the noise somehow could change the situation. She tried the knob. The paper dropped along the molding like the blade of a guillotine. A strange excitement gripped her. She plucked up the note and carried it inside.

His room was messy—probably the norm, she guessed, taking it as a compliment; twice a week for class, everything was always clean and tidy, meaning Julian made a special effort on her account. She looked around. An open closet door revealed his wardrobe—a crowded row of whitewashed arms and pant legs. Why, she wondered, did he have to call attention to himself that way? Sister Zoë had told her he was famous. You had to know about chess, of course, but those who did knew Julian. Maybe he thought of his clothes as a kind of costume. A heap of them lay in the corner beside his bed. What a muddle. He did not sleep well, she could tell. The sheets and pillows looked like they had been strangled.

A row of snapshots caught her eye. She did not recall their being there before. Girls. Two were portraits, wallet-sized, each changed in some sarcastic way. He had used a felt-tipped pen to make the eyes go crossed on one, and had drawn a mustache on the other. A little to the left there was a third. Naked! Melanie turned her eyes away, embarrassed. The lady pictured was bending down, smiling, peeking around her shoulder, her fingers spreading open her behind. In a bubble drawn above her head, "No Exit" had been written. Melanie wanted to scratch the image from the wall, tear it into shreds. She got up in a huff from the bed (where she had been kneeling), all primed to leave, but once more her attention was arrested.

On the wall adjacent, two more bits of Julian's memorabilia were affixed. She was half-afraid to look; there was another photograph. But this one was un-defaced, its subject clothed—a female, older, maybe forty, a handsome woman with auburn hair, pink lips, and sea-green eyes. His mother? There was scarcely a resemblance. Yet something in the features looked familiar, looked like Julian—an aspect more than anything specific.

Next to it was a clipping from a newspaper. Its caption read:

Chess Wiz Loses By Default

Melanie moved closer.

Local chess prodigy Julian Papp, after playing brilliantly through forty-two moves in his exhibition match with visiting Grandmaster Alexander Geokov, was forced to discontinue due to sudden illness, thereby conceding defeat for the first time in his phenomenal career. Yesterday's challenge marked the twelfth time Mr. Papp had taken on a world-ranked player. His previously unbroken string of victories, in combination with his unorthodox play, was legendary.

Asked to comment on the unexpectedly abrupt cessation of the contest, Mr. Geokov said, 'The boy plays very well for an amateur.'

This last line had been underscored with the felt-tipped pen three times.

Melanie, feeling a twinge of conscience at having spied on his private things, hesitated at the door, listened, then slipped out.

* * *

'Mrs. Papp?'

'This is Sister Zoë at St. Francis.'

'Julian has been missing since yesterday. We weren't aware of this until an hour ago... Mrs. Papp?... Mrs. Papp?'

'I know you're concerned. We all are, too. But I don't think we should assume the worst. This is not another suicide attempt. You can rest assured of that. He left no note. He has not had any recent seizures. He has not been seriously depressed.'

'Of course not, Mrs. Papp. Now please calm down.'

'We think he was caught out in a storm and had to find some shelter. We've had heavy snowfall overnight, and again all day today. Julian was seen leaving the grounds Friday morning about ten o'clock. All his things are in his room so it does not appear as if he's run away. But he has been known to take extended walks.'

'Mrs. Papp, you'll do neither Julian nor yourself any good by getting overwrought.'

'Well, as I said, we've had a lot of snow. The main roads have been closed so we're very much cut off right now.'

'Let me finish. Of course the Highway Patrol has been alerted, as has the Forest Service. There are a number of observation towers in our area from which a campfire might be seen. Visibility has been poor, though, so we've heard nothing yet. But I assure you, Mrs. Papp, everything that can be done, we are doing.'

'Search parties would do no good until this storm has passed.'

'Mrs. Papp, he could be three feet away from a would-be rescuer and not be seen in this blizzard. It is senseless even to try until the snow lets up. And senseless to speculate about morbid possibilities. There are summer cabins in the area. There are some abandoned mines, some caves. Your son is bright, resourceful. There are as many reasons for hope as for despair—more, in fact. Now, as to your coming, I can hardly object. If you feel you must, by all means come. But I should warn you that it may prove far more frustrating than staying at home. As I have said, the roads are closed. There's no telling when they'll be reopened. You could be sitting in a lonely hotel room for days just waiting. That is, *if* the airport itself is open. On the other hand, the phone lines, obviously, are clear. I can keep you abreast of everything as it happens. Again, it's up to you. I just think it would be far worse to put yourself through all the trauma and expense of traveling under these conditions.'

There was a pause during which the nun hoped Mrs. Papp would reconsider. Everything she had told the woman was true. A visit now would serve no useful purpose.

'I understand. Any mother would feel the same. What's important is that we keep our heads.'

'Now, if I may suggest, call a friend—a close friend—and have her come and stay with you tonight. I promise you I'll phone the minute that I hear. According to the latest weather forecast, the skies are due to clear sometime tomorrow. Until then, there's really nothing any of us can do. I know it's useless to say, "don't worry," but I tell you frankly, Mrs. Papp, I believe your son is okay. We've had many crises at St. Francis through the years, and in every case I've had a feeling when one was going to turn out badly. I have not had that feeling this time. I believe your son, like all of us, is simply waiting out the storm.'

'I pray, too. Prayer is always helpful. Now do as I suggest and call that friend. And please, try to be patient. We ourselves are relying on the phone for information; it's important that we don't tie up the line.'

'Expect to hear from me tomorrow.'

'Yes?'

'I'll call tomorrow. Goodnight.'

* * *

Since Father Ring had not gotten through, Sunday

morning Mass could not be said. An offering, instead, was made toward Julian's safe return—prospects for which grew bleaker with each mounting inch of snow. Even Sister Zoë's peculiar optimism paled. She led the prayers herself, a more than able stand-in for the priest, Father Ring—righteous, stern, respectable, and hopelessly unimaginative. Not unlike the Church, which still refused to ordain women—another bone of contention in Sister Zoë's unorthodox theology. So much dogma, laid down so long ago, long before the Lord's apologists had had the dimmest glimmerings of the equity of souls.

She looked across the congregation's prayer-bowed heads. Could people but perceive that all were equal in the eyes of God, that "male" and "female" were not spiritual distinctions but merely physical ones—a single chromosome's difference—how drastically the world would change... and the nun could not help thinking it might change "for the better." She sighed. Actually, it was not the long-familiar blight of chauvinism about which she was worried. A patient had been missing for close to forty-seven hours, thirty-six without her even knowing. Had only she not relaxed the surveillance or insisted that Julian keep coming for his pills. But no, she had given orders to Sister Clara to discontinue watching, and the medication was now in Julian's hands.

The voices of the faithful sang. If it seemed at times that prayer went unheard, she knew God always listened to these psalms. They were so beautiful. The notes rose, floating to the heights like liberated bits of light. Music changed the nature of the air, making it a medium through which the Word could effortlessly travel.

Coats were rustled. The few who had braved the weather lassoed collars with their scarves. Boots were snapped, zipped, or buckled. The chapel doors were opened with a howling rush of frosted wind. And the nuns plus patients, in single file, departed... leaving Sister Zoë alone.

'Dear Lord, I am Thy servant; deeply flawed, yet ever willing to tread the path Thy loving Light has clearly shown. Thou speakest to me in words that have no letter, in sentences devoid of sound, teaching me to listen as one listens for a pulse, through touch. I throb with joy whenever I comprehend Thy holy Meaning. Lord, this day, I humbly ask for guidance. A child is lost, a child of Thine, whose life I fear has still too many questions left unasked, too many unanswered. Please bless our search, dear Lord, and, if it be Thy will, let him be found.'

She crossed herself, genuflected, and left her prayer to echo in the omnipresent Consciousness of her Maker.

* * *

A roof overhead, a warming fire, coffee, and a chessboard—thus Julian was ensconced in a warp of time. Two nights had come and gone unnoticed. The snow had deepened. But like the hourglass on the hearth, internal time, for Julian, had settled to a quintessential halt.

He was not inactive, however. True, there was a stillness akin to meditative states, a harmony, a oneness. This, however, was balanced by intensive mental diligence in the form of concentration on the game—innumerable games. He played himself, ego vs. alter ego. It was a schizophrenic exercise he had developed as a child when his talent had outclassed all of the competition's. The challenge lay in each mind's knowing everything about its twin, and move by move inventing ever-escalating schemes—to outmaneuver Black, to hoodwink White. The discipline required to keep from favoring one side over the other was immense. Yet that was steadfastly the rule. He never broke it. Though often it was tempting—especially when the split had gone too far. He had read a story once about a man who had done just that, allowed his dualistic play to usurp his sanity. That challenge loomed presently, for psychological stability was every bit as crucial as one's knowledge of the game. Control! Self-mastery trumped twofold! The stakes were high, but so were the rewards. For when he could hold his own against himself without a nervous break, the game was indescribably exhilarating. When not, he forced his arm to clear the board.

On occasion, he had slept, dreamlessly. For the first time since the nightmares started, he had been unafraid to close his eyes. The bed, so fragrant from the pine, had enveloped him as with a Lethean calm, delivering him afresh upon each waking.

It was what? Sunday morning? The logs with which he had fed the fire were spent. He had stubble on his cheeks. The kettle needed heating. He scratched his head with both hands vigorously, stretched and yawned, then shivered from the unchecked cold. Wood, more wood.

He looked for his sneakers. They stood turned out before the fireplace, tongues gone rigid, laces stiff, in a comic state of lolling rigor mortis. At least they were dry. He broke them to his feet, put on his sweater, his dark glasses, and opened the cabin door. A drift of snow, conforming to the threshold, held its flat-faced windswept shape. The scene beyond was dazzlingly, blindingly bright. Even with his glasses on, Julian had to squint. The sun was making prisms of the icicles, rainbow colors splayed across the snow—virgin snow, pure, the whitest white, spreading out in all directions like a knee-deep frozen topping. The path he had shoveled to the outhouse once again lay buried, a gentle swell to either side indicating his toil.

He felt a playful urge to be the first to mark the untrodden plane, leave a wake of carefree tracks for other, less courageous souls to follow. Except it would help to know which way to head. He reviewed his predicament. Firstly, they would be looking for him. Three days AWOL was bound to have drawn attention. And after everyone expressed relief that he had managed to survive, he knew the reprimands would fly hot and heavy.

He would worry about that later. The chief thing was to find his way. With the landscape's blizzard-changed appearance, and without his former footprints as a guide, that would not be easy. The drifts would make it even tougher. At least he need not start out unprepared. He could take some food, matches, a blanket maybe.

He checked the sky. This break in the weather might not last. Perhaps he had best make ready to take his leave.

* * *

Throughout the sanitarium, speculation was rife about the chess player's disappearance. The usual explanations for a patient's sudden absence—discharge or demise—would hardly have caused a stir. "Missing", however, was a rare, almost exotic category—with Mr. Papp's reclusiveness contributing to the general curiosity. No one really knew him. Opinions, thus, were prone to the most ridiculous hypotheses, in accordance with their spokesmen's misconceptions, ranging from, "He's run away to Flagstaff hoping to get himself a decent meal," to, "He returned to the ghostly haunts of the walking dead"— this latter from "Stone-deaf Seth," St. Francis's oldest and least endearing resident. But of all the reactions, one stood out as being the most distressed, the most profound: Melanie's.

She sat in her room alone, her sketchbook in her lap, struggling to express her dismal emptiness. She felt cut off, abandoned. And lonely. And angry at his obvious indifference. He had left without a word to her, as though she scarcely mattered. Where had he gone, anyway? Was he lost? He was too smart for that. She was half convinced his exit was deliberate, and a personal affront to her. So what if she did have to cancel one measly class? Was that any reason to run away and hide? Besides, she hadn't cancelled it; she had been there right on time.

The pressure made her charcoal snap on another of her portraits, another one of him. She had amassed quite a collection: Julian looking condescending, Julian looking mean, Julian poised to make a chess move, Julian pointing at her hair, Julian somber, Julian sad. And now this latest—Julian left unfinished. She tossed the sketchbook on the bed. His cheek and chin and lower lip, part of his forehead, and one umbrageous lens of his dark glasses, lay facing, indistinctly, toward the ceiling.

She looked out the window. A team of searchers was wearily returning. She strained to see if Julian was among them. No. Like all the others throughout the day, they trudged back empty-handed.

The sky was breeding clouds. Another storm was due. It was getting dark. What if he really was out there lost, or maybe worse? The way he dressed, he would not have lasted long. This would be the third night. And what about his seizures? She knew he needed medicine every day. What if he had left his pills behind?

Large flakes began to fall again. They drifted slowly, steadily, reclaiming the footprints tramped below. The volatile emotions she had experienced of late recommenced with a pang of mortal fear. What if…

Like the spectral figure of hooded Death, Julian appeared. His step was plodding. His frozen pant legs knocked against his shins. Clutched about him, a blanket trailed two rigid flaps that scrawled twin indentations in the snow. They wound down through a stand of pine like paralleling skis.

Her heart was racing. He was real again.

The impressions she had fashioned in his absence, pro and con, seemed merely fantastical compared to this, his actual return. All her apprehensions returned as well. There was something ominous about this man. As he drew near, in the failing light, his silhouette looked hauntingly foreboding. Secrets lurked inside that cold-stiffened shroud, secrets she might never want to learn.

Her cheeks grew flushed. The window clouded over with her breath. Nervously, she wiped it clear. He had reached the common. There he paused. He turned his shadowed face in the direction of her room. Attracted and repelled, Melanie stood suspended in anticipation. Then, just when she decided it was not at her he peered, off flew the blanket cape-like, and Julian—grinning smugly— performed, with mock-civility, a courtly bow.

She jerked the curtains closed.

* * *

'So Mother Dear has been "in touch" again?'

'Quite understandable under the circumstances, don't you think?'

'Oh, quite. I'm surprised she isn't here. You *did* discourage her from coming to the rescue?'

'I did my best.'

'Fine. Good. Now back to the point: I want to quit the medication.'

'That's absolutely out…'

'Let me finish. I've been two days without it and haven't had a seizure or a nightmare. I know that doesn't mean

I'm cured; I'm not that optimistic. It does, however, seem to suggest that the drugs induce the wretched dream.'

'There may be…'

'The gist of which I'm about to tell you. I've wanted to before, but up till now, it's been a jumble. I've had time, though, to sort things out. And Melanie is the key.'

'Melanie?'

'The dream is about her, not me.'

'I see.'

'Sounds crazy, I know. But hear me out, at least.'

'I wasn't being judgmental. Go ahead.'

'You'll correct me if I get things wrong?'

'Wrong? How would I…'

'About Melanie's case.'

'Julian, I've told you before, I will not discuss…'

'I'm not asking you to discuss it—not yet, anyway. Just tell me whether what I say is true or false. Based on what you know. Otherwise, there's no way I can prove I've not gone mad. Agreed?'

The risk of betraying one patient's confidence on the basis of another's dream seemed small—especially when so little of Melanie's past was actually known. And even if, by chance, a fact or two should be involved, the issue, in the nun's mind, was Julian not Melanie. His refusing medication was a serious decision, a mistake. What confidence he had recently recovered could be lost if he fell victim to another bout of seizures. Better to allay his fears by letting him give vent to his (alleged) recurrent dream.

'Okay, agreed.'

'Mostly there are men's voices; three, I think. None of them speaks to me. I'm only an eavesdropper. That's one of the uncanny things about the dream; I'm totally detached. The dialogue goes on regardless, like it would if I weren't there. I can't recite what's said; I don't remember. And that's another puzzling thing. I don't remember. I can tell you about dreams I had when I was five, in full detail. Why this one is an exception, I don't know. It has to be the drugs. Which isn't to say I'm spinning you a fairy tale. What I have been able to recall is real. Accurate, I mean. It's just not comprehensive. They're crude, they're violent, and they're rapists.'

The nun had not expected this. And though she affected calm, she knew her surprise had registered—and that Julian, of course, had noticed.

'So it's true?'

'What's true, Julian?'

'That Melanie was raped?'

She felt he had trapped her. How could he have known? Was he guessing? Was he using the pretext of this dream to wheedle information she had denied him? The thought occurred that his dream itself might be a fabrication, a device that he had concocted to achieve some private end. What end, though? She knew Melanie was somehow important to him. But this was so implausible a scheme—if it were a scheme. Was he lying? She thought not. Yet she could not overcome the sense that Julian was trying to manipulate her.

He waited patiently for her answer.

'Yes, it is true.'

'So that's the thing she can't—or won't—remember. It's no wonder, I should think. What's the situation now?'

'With Melanie?'

'Or Marcy, as the case may be.'

'She's quite herself again.'

'I'm glad to hear that. By the way, what caused her "minor setback?"'

'I agreed I would listen to your dream, not answer questions about Melanie.'

'But they're inseparable.'

'In your mind, perhaps.'

'I resent that.'

'Listen, Julian. How this girl's unfortunate ordeal has found its way into your subconscious, only you can tell. But I sincerely doubt your medication is to blame. It may affect the frequency with which you dream, but certainly not the content.'

'Then how would *you* explain my little nightmare?'

'Frankly?'

'Be my guest.'

'I would say that you gained this information consciously, and through guilt about *how* it was obtained, you locked it into your subconscious.'

'How moralistic. Do I detect a hint of accusation?'

He knew the nun was groping in the dark. She had no proof. Besides, his espionage had simply evened the odds. There was no need to feel guilty.

'Perhaps this matter is best resolved by calling it "coincidence."'

The nun's dismissing it thus was hardly satisfactory, however. That he indeed had used "irregular" means to learn the facts did not explain the nightmare's authenticity. It was all still much too vague.

There were but a few things more he could relate, besides his intuition that the dream was not a dream per se. But in exploiting the subject, he realized he had lost his chance to hear the nun's opinion. Her "adversary status" (which he knew he had imposed himself) prejudiced whatever she might say. How to plumb her expertise without relinquishing his slim advantage? Mentally he shifted gears. The nun's black habit became a field of sixty-four squares, half of their ranks white. He peopled them with Pawns, Rooks, Bishops, Queens, Kings, and the last two Knights—which had yet to be exchanged.

With a blink, the pattern disassembled.

'For the sake of argument, let's grant I do know something about her history.'

'Obtained?'

'Surreptitiously, of course. Let's say Ms. Dana told me.'

'I can't believe…'

'Too farfetched? We're only hypothesizing. Well, let's say, then, I pilfered Melanie's file—have it stashed away somewhere. Under my pillow. Now, with such a source of comprehensive data resting nightly under my head, do you think it likely my imagination could take those facts—through osmosis, if you like—and manufacture circumstances into which they'd fit?'

Was Julian confessing? He must have seen the file. She had difficulty reading him, this man behind the poker-face façade. Why did he persist in all these bluffs, feints, and stratagems?

'Julian, what's the point?'

He thought a moment. She had him there. Maybe the dream *was* spawned by a guilty conscious.

'A black van with a fisheye window.'

'I beg your pardon; what?'

He had studied her reaction closely. The image had not rung a bell. Perhaps the nun knew nothing about the rape. Perhaps his own extrapolations could only be corroborated or dispelled by Melanie herself. And *that* was the point—one of them, at least. He had to find a rational explanation for the dream, before it recurred. The exchange would have to wait. The nun apparently had nothing more to offer.

'Skip it, Ms. Zoë—"an undigested bit of beef."'

He rose to go.

'Just a minute, Julian. What about your medicine?'

He took the bottle from his pocket and set it on her desk.

'Here. I told you, I'm trying to kick.'

'And I told you, autonomy is not the way of it here, especially for one who just caused such an uproar. Need I remind you that this entire county was searching for a man who "simply took a little stroll?" Sit down!'

He did.

'Honestly, Julian, you amaze me. It's bad enough you haven't offered an account—not to mention an apology— but then to say blithely that you've decided not to take the medication we prescribe, is tantamount to…'

'Blasphemy?'

'No, disrespect! Blatant, arrogant, ignorant disrespect! Your epilepsy is *treatable*, not curable. The seizures *will* resume. And the responsibility for that is *yours*. Accept it, and give the rest of us some credit. We're not fools, you know. Don't let conceit deprive you of a helping hand; we all can use one every now and then.'

She shook the proper dosage from the pill container and held it out to him.

'Please. You wear those glasses to protect your eyes; willpower doesn't make the light less painful. Let the drugs protect you, too.'

It looked incongruous to him, almost sinister—this "representative of heaven" pushing pills. And yet he could not help believing that she cared. It was touching, even. Was she right, though? Were his nightmares and these anticonvulsants unrelated? He looked at the tablets.

He plucked them from her palm, popped them into his mouth, and slowly chewed.

With the insides of her mouth constricting sympathetically, Sister Zoë winced.

'How *can* you do that? Oh, swallow. Swallow, please!'

He gulped and grinned.

'Must do penance before receiving grace.'

She shook her head, holding out the bottle.

'Here, take them with you.'

'You mean you still trust me? Why Ms. Zoë, I'm truly flattered.'

'I've simply lost my nerve—almost my dinner.'

'Which reminds me, I could use a bite to eat. We're through?'

'I have your promise to obey the curfew?'

'Sure.'

'You will take the pills?'

'Provisionally.'

'And these walks of yours will be henceforth curtailed?'

'Abridged.'

'All right, then. You may go.'

* * *

Snuggled up in the corner of her bed with all the pillows, sheets, and blankets tucked around her, Melanie sat, knees to her chest, thinking. The nerve he had, disappearing for three whole days without an explanation! Sister Dana had filled her in on Julian's "miraculous" return—no frostbite, thirst, or hunger—carrying that woolen blanket from who knows where. Obviously, he had found some shelter. Obviously, his "dire distress" had not been that at all. But he refused to give the scantiest detail. Just like him, too. Sister Zoë reportedly had scolded him, and, in Sister Dana's version, Mr. Papp, at last, was duly humbled. Melanie found that difficult to believe, however.

She nestled deeper. Tuesday. She had Chess today at two o'clock. Hours away. The sun was not even up yet. She had wanted to see him all day Monday. Instead, she had done another drawing—Julian making that comic-opera bow. She had made sure to show the stupid grin he had grinned, and just for fun (and to get back at him a little) she had put him in a jester's cap. Served him right.

She leaned her chin against her knees, hugging her

legs tightly, rocking slowly. Julian. The bed felt nice and cozy and warm. And wet? She pulled back the covers and lifted her gown to see. A bloodstain spread from between her legs. For a moment she held very still. Her periods, though irregular, had not caused any problems since her injuries had healed. But now, this rust-colored spot beneath her seemed like a wound reopened.

'No!'

Her legs snapped closed. She rushed into the bathroom.

Tuesday, November 11th, at 6:06 in the A.M. I almost remembered something. It was right at the tip of my tongue, that close. I almost had it. Then it was gone. Everybody thinks I forget on purpose. That's not true. I try. I just can't remember stuff. I probably have brain damage or something.

I haven't seen Julian since he came back. He makes me so mad I could scream. He could have come to see me. He doesn't care, though. He doesn't care about anyone but himself. He wouldn't even tell Sister where he was all that time. She had practically the whole state out looking for him and he just strutted back, all on his own, as if what he did was nobody else's business. At least he got hollered at. Sister gave it to him good. Sister Dana told me that. Except she dislikes Julian so much she might have exaggerated. Why should I care, though? So what if he's teaching me chess? He's probably doing that for one of his selfish reasons, too.

I wandered around all day yesterday taking turns liking him *and hating him. Stupid. I wish I could figure out why he's on my mind all the time. Not knowing makes me nervous. I do not have a crush on him. That's kid's stuff. "He's merely a fascinating young man in whom I'm taking a temporary interest." That's how <u>he</u> sounds. I wonder how come? He wants people to think he's smart, I suppose. And he is. Though you'd think a person with all his brains would be a little happier.*

She closed the journal and dressed. Maybe he was up and having coffee. He rarely was in the cafeteria at normal times. So, if you wanted to come across him (accidentally, of course), it was best to choose unusual spots and hours.

Melanie made her way to the cafeteria.

***

He had not slept. He had pounded and kicked at the cafeteria doors before the girl would open, then he lied (claiming "special permission") before he could get some service. Nursing solemnly his third refill of coffee, he watched as Melanie crossed the snowy common—bounding through the drifts like a frisky colt, her breath puffed silver. Inwardly, he groaned. He did not relish anybody's company just now, especially this eager young girl's, whose presence (for she undoubtedly was cantering his way) could only serve to churn conflicting emotions. Besides, he had suffered another seizure. He suspected it had been a mild one—he had not fallen, nor were there any signs he had thrashed about—just a little reminder that his body and his mind were not his own.

Melanie was knocking at the double doors. The cafeteria attendant went to answer.

'Sorry. We're not open until seven.'

Melanie looked beyond her.

'What about him?'

The girl looked blankly, apparently not considering Julian's being there a contradiction—or grounds for relaxing the rules a second time.

'I'm sorry.'

Melanie scowled.

'Julian, this girl won't let me in!'

He looked over, paused long enough to make her angry, then motioned it would be okay. The girl let Melanie enter. She marched directly over to his table.

'Thank you, Your Highness. God, you'd think you owned the place.'

He made no reply.

'Aren't you going to ask me to sit down?'

He remained silent.

Should she join him uninvited? Or should she turn on her heels and storm out for good?

He arrested the latter course by a grudging nod.

Melanie sat down.

'You look awful. What's the matter?'

'Awful? Worse than usual, you mean? Here, have a closer look.'

He removed his glasses.

Recovering from the shock of this unprecedented action, Melanie noted the condition of Julian's eyes. They looked positively ghoulish, bloodshot, rimmed with sallow skin, the irises ablaze with gory color. But her inspection quickly changed from looking *at* his eyes, to looking *into* them. He bore this with a mixture of nostalgia and despair. He had seen before what he described as "the evangelic look." In Miriam. What saddened him was its being aped by Melanie—whom he had considered a different breed, unique in certain respects. And perhaps she was indeed, for presently she made him look away—something Miriam had never made him do.

'Petitioning my soul?'

He moved to replace his glasses. Impulsively, she intercepted his hand.

'Don't. Please? Unless it hurts. Is the light too bright here?'

Her gesture had surprised them both. He hesitated, unsure why. She held his hand, frightened, yet unwilling to let it go.

'No... No, the light's all right... I knew a girl once

who fancied herself a soul-gazer—one Miriam Jeffries, by name. A pathetic case was Miriam. She…'

His words trailed off. Melanie's eyes were embarrassing him. He averted his own a second time. She sensed his shyness, and would have stopped, had not she felt a strange connection, or a sensation actually, a tingly sort of vibration in her spine, which she had felt before, though not as strongly as now. With their palms together, touching, Julian felt it, too—or something similar. He let his eyes return to hers. For a moment longer, each allowed the other a fundamental probing.

Then the contact of their hands made both self-conscious. Simultaneously they flinched and broke the bridge; the strange communion ended.

Neither had a ready explanation, though Melanie now appeared the more confused.

'Julian, I… You…'

He sought to cover.

'Ms. Miriam Jeffries, I was saying, a real crusader. Miriam believed in Karma—and Zen and Christ and Yoga and Palmistry and a bastard version of Reincarnation, and half a dozen other things. I was David to her Bathsheba, until it all went sour. Then she moved on to become St. Joan—recasting me Nebuchadnezzar. Have you ever noticed how the past-life preachers always trace their lines to people who are famous—or infamous?'

'What happened to her?'

'I think she married Robin Hood and started breeding merry men.'

She laughed. He had not heard her laugh before. It had a pleasant sound. He liked it, and it helped relieve the tension. Suddenly, she grew sullen.

'Have you had a lot of girl friends?'

'Just the ones you saw tacked on my wall.'

She blushed. How had he known? She hastened to deny it.

'I don't know what you're talking about.'

He reached into his pocket and presented her with a piece of folded paper. It was her note. He read:

'Bishop to e6. Check. King to…'

'Where did you get that?'

'Where you left it for me, of course. Down the crack between my bed and pin-up wall.'

How humiliating! She tried to fashion an acceptable excuse, borrowing from the truth.

'I was just coming to class, is all. I knocked and you didn't answer so I went in to leave you a note.'

'Thinking I'd be sure to see it hidden under the bed.'

'I didn't put it there on purpose. I must have dropped it accidentally.'

'While you were straightening up for me? How sweet.'

She got mad. Why did he have to drag it out, make her suffer?

'You just want to make me feel bad because I saw your nasty pictures. You're the one who ought to be ashamed.'

'I guess you didn't like my gallery. No wonder, they *are* an ugly crew.'

'Because you made them that way!'

'It's true. I seem to bring out the worst in people—case in point.'

'You know what I mean.'

'Oh, my modifications? Believe me, those are vast improvements. The originals have deformities that far exceed the whimsies of my pen. Shall I enumerate them? From left to right we had: Polly Elton, a pearl of a girl, faithful and true-blue, who…'

'Don't bother. I'm not interested.'

'No? Then why were you over there ogling them? Polly Elton, I say—my first—a moon-faced sort of doting type whose freckles gave me hours of unadulterated joy— I told her, you see, that if she let me lick them, I could make them disappear. I think at first she half believed me. Perhaps that early disappointment preordained our end. She up and left me for another—who either didn't tell white lies, or was a better licker.'

'Julian, I know you're trying to be funny, but…'

'Then came Miriam, the girl I mentioned. I neglected, though, to tell you why we failed to get along. It wasn't her affinity for aberrant beliefs, so much as her aversion toward anatomy—especially mine. The simple maxim, "in our bodies do our souls reside"—when faced with my integument—was much too much for Miriam. We parted chastely, leaving not a mark one another's hide.'

Melanie got up to leave.

'And now we come to the champion of them all—Mercedes Ballantine.'

She put on her coat, hat, and gloves, then paused to see if he would stop.

'Mercedes—she from whom, once suckered in, I was granted no reprieve.'

Melanie started to go.

'She saw me win a challenge match last year. Or was it two years ago? No matter; her impact stays the same. She was struck by the disparity between my age and that of my opponent, imagining me a babe-in-arms—her arms—which were long and graceful and, like her legs, tentacular. She had an intriguing theory about genius. Mercedes believed it could be sucked, like an egg yolk, through a pinhole in its shell. Equipped herself with a special beak for piercing people's shells, Mercedes made a hobby out of sodomizing eggs—prize eggs, that is.'

This was too much. Melanie had heard enough. And yet she had to force herself to walk away.

'I don't think the woman knew a thing about the game. She was there with a musician—a famous one, I gathered. *He* was the chess-buff; she just tagged along for sundry kicks. I guess he had given a pretty glowing account of me, because after the match she came fluttering around like a moth, a regal moth—or a bitch in heat. That was her unique allure—a compelling combination of Divine Right Queen and whore. She invited me to a dinner party.'

Having reached the cafeteria doors (Julian not quite beyond her hearing), Melanie hesitated.

'I admit I was flattered. She was gorgeous, and sophisticated. No question she had money. And as I said, she absolutely reeked of sex. So I showed up at the appointed hour, flowers in hand, a lamb for slaughter.'

She gripped the handle to release its latch but did not depress it.

'The desk-clerk in the lobby phoned, announcing my arrival. Fifth floor, room number 508. The elevator opened, I stepped in, pressed five, the doors slid closed, and I was born up bliss-ward, unresisting.'

Julian, looking straight ahead at no one, took a sip of coffee.

'The carpet in the hallway sported fleur-de-lis. There was a peephole in the door. I felt her peering. I peered back and saw a nose and one distorted mascaraed eye. It winked. The door swung open. And there she stood—a blood-red smile across her face, stark naked.'

He took another sip.

'I gasped. She laughed, and pulled me in. There was no dinner—or rather, *I* was dinner. She excused her bold appearance in a toast—"I examined you," she said, "It's only fair I grant you equal time." We clicked glasses. The wine, I'm sure, was drugged. And from that point on, the evening was a psychedelic whir.'

His coffee was cold and bitter as he took another swallow.

'When I got home my mother nearly fainted. I was covered, head to foot, in eyebrow-penciled lines, looking like some necromantic diagram. All the symbols were colored with rouge, foundation, hair dye, and some twenty different shades of high-gloss lipstick. She had to bathe me; I was in no condition to bathe myself. I remember watching this gaudy oil slick swirling down the drain— along with my self-respect. Next day I went back. She had checked out. The desk clerk had an envelope for me. I hoped it was her forwarding address. Instead it held a photograph—Mercedes in the nude, bending over, cheeks—both sets—composed in mocking smiles.'

He downed the remainder of his coffee.

'The snapshot had an inscription on the back. It read: "To my dear vanilla puppy, you were delicious. Many happy returns, ha-ha, Mercedes."'

Finally Melanie depressed the handle and left.

Julian, following with his eyes, repeated 'ha ha.'

* * *

'So where are you now?'

'And you can't get through?'

'Who won't?'

'Mesa? But that's almost back to Phoenix.'

'I tried to all evening Sunday; your line was busy.'

'Oh, I am sorry, Mrs. Papp. If you had only waited. I phoned you back the minute I knew that Julian was safe. It couldn't have been an hour after your call.'

'Of course, I understand.'

Sister Dana entered. Sister Zoë motioned to her to sit and serve herself some tea.

'The plows are out. All you really can do is wait. I don't think it will take too long.'

She mouthed, "Julian's mother."

'He's probably in his room. I can ask him to return your call. What's your number?'

She signaled Sister Dana to take down the number.

'Yes. Five five five—three two eight eight.'

'No, I think it's clear for the moment.'

'Later this afternoon, then?'

'How about two o'clock?'

'I'll make… Yes, I promise. One of us for certain will return your call.'

'Goodbye.'

The old nun sighed and slumped back in her chair.

'That was Philomena Papp. Calling us from Payson.'

'Payson? You mean she's here in Arizona, on her way to St. Francis?'

'On her way if she could be. She's snowed in, thank goodness.'

'Why do you say that?'

'It gives us time—I hope enough time—to dissuade her. I fear she is going to petition us for Julian's release.'

Good riddance, the young nun thought but did not say aloud—though Sister Zoë reacted otherwise.

'What is this animosity I sense between you and Julian Papp? What has he done to you, Sister Dana, to earn this hardness in your heart?'

It was an unfair question, the young nun felt. She was disinclined to answer. There were people one just did not take to, and for her "Mr. Papp" was in that category. Maybe it was his arrogance, or his snide sarcastic quips. Or maybe it was the way he stared at a person, psychologically undressing her. He seemed to know a person's secret weaknesses. Worse, he seemed to know how to exploit them. And worst of all, he was an evil influence on her ward. But before Sister Dana could revise her hatred in terms of the need to safeguard Melanie, a knock resounded mightily on the outer door.

'Good morning, Sister Zoë, Sister Dana. Excuse my interrupting.'

'Sister Agatha. What a pleasant surprise. Come in, sit down.'

'No, I'm sorry, I can't stay. I only came to tell you that I just sewed eleven stitches into Julian Papp's right hand.'

'Oh, dear.'

'And that he is one of the most insolent, ill-mannered, irreverent, uncouth, exasperating individuals it has ever been my solemn duty to treat!'

'Oh, dear, oh, dear. What happened?'

The irate nurse proceeded with a blow-by-blow account (after which Sister Dana felt quite justified in resting her case).

Within half an hour, Julian was standing on the very spot where he had been defamed.

'I have just been informed that you paid a call on our infirmary.'

He un-pocketed his bandaged hand and held it up.

'Hunting accident.'

'Oh? You told Sister Agatha you had been bitten by the Holy Ghost.'

'Just trying to raise their spirits at the morgue.'

He grinned. She did not.

'So you were hunting; may I ask what?'

'Rabbit—the elusive snowshoe hare. I saw one this morning, nose twitching, crouching in my bathroom mirror. I approached on tiptoe, froze him with a stare, and dispatched him with a shattering karate chop.'

'I see. I was unaware that rabbit was in season.'

'Opened yesterday.'

'And closes today. Another seizure, Julian?'

He nodded.

'Severe?'

'I don't think so. How did you know?'

'I expected as much when I heard how "charming" you had been to Sister Agatha. Please, sit down.'

Dropping his jacket on the chair, he broke precedent and sat down on the couch. The nun came from behind her desk and joined him. She was concerned. His mood was dark. The humor with which he guarded himself was stretched conspicuously thin. And for the first time since he had been admitted, Julian seemed vulnerable— dangerously so.

A silence fell between them, which they both respected.

Finally the nun began.

'Your mother phoned. She wants to come and see you.'

This, of course, he had expected. His answer was prepared. But his interest in the phantom Game momentarily flagged.

He simply nodded.

'I have promised her that we would return her call. At two. Would you please be here?'

He did not respond.

'She didn't learn that you were safe until this morning. Perhaps you'll fill her in on where you went.'

'When even you couldn't grill it out of me? Not likely.'

'Isn't your mother more persuasive?'

'My mother...'

He broke off.

'Yes, go on... Julian, you haven't told me how you feel about her coming.'

'Indifferently.'

'Will you tell her about this latest seizure?'

'Afraid I'll smear your reputation?'

'You sound angry.'

'Of course I'm angry. I haven't slept, I look like hell, my playing hand's been maimed, and to top things off I've had another goddamn fit! If Mother Dear were to get one look at me, I'm gone.'

'So you're worried she might ask for your release?'

'*Demand*, Ms. Zoë, *demand*. My mother may be wishy-washy where *her* life is concerned, but when it comes to mine the woman is tough as nails. I'd be out of here in a matter of minutes, mark my words.'

The move was made in spite of himself—a reflex. The Queen's threat had to be removed. Sister Zoë obliged.

'Julian, I promise, the decision to go or stay rests entirely with you. Even if your mother were to insist, I don't want you to feel you're under any pressure.'

Dictates of The Game appeased, he let his mind sink back into its depression.

'I don't think it will happen, though. Your mother has put her trust in our approach. I doubt she would change her mind.'

He stirred himself.

'In the face of all the "progress" that we've made?'

'Yes, "we've" made. I'm glad you said it. That's evidence enough. All I've heard since you first came is "I" and "They"—Julian versus The World. You've been treating us like opponents. But I believe that may be changing. I believe you've come to realize that people here are on your side, not only willing but capable of helping you.'

'All that, from a slip of the tongue? Amazing.'

'I'm wrong, then? You would rather leave?'

'I didn't say that. I admit I need a little break from hearth and home—I'll be here at two—but allow me some integrity. I have to play this game out on my own.'

Game! Sister Zoë knew that this game business was precisely the problem. He insisted on perceiving things in terms of competition. She wanted to take Julian by the shoulders and shake him—then hug him, for he needed that even more. He looked smaller, somehow, slouching in the corner of her couch. He was not very big—no more than 5 feet 6, slight of build.

Seeing him so closely, however, the nun could well imagine how, in ancient times, albinos (and suchlike) were revered. Often looked upon as holy men, oracles, or seers, they were worshipfully pampered in the courts of emperors and kings. She had a sudden urge to touch him— of which she felt immediately ashamed, for it seemed to spring from some remote and dusky superstition.

Then all that seemed quite silly. His injured hand was resting near. Surely there was nothing that prevented her from examining it, casually. Yet as she reached, he flinched, as though he sensed the root of her intention. He was glaring at her, or rather, his coal-black lenses were. How their blind expressionlessness framed such vivid import she had no idea, but she felt distinctly indicted by their stare.

'Is it painful? Our nurse said that the cut was fairly deep.'

He expelled a hollow laugh.

'I'll live.'

'Had you intended otherwise?... Julian?'

'"All that dies is our reflection." Isn't that a quote from something?'

'I don't know. Will you tell me what it means?'

'You're the immortality buff. How would you explain it?'

'I would say it meant our shell is all that dies—the ego we have mistaken for our essence.'

'And I suppose this "essence," once its envelope drops dead, wings its way to Heaven or goes plummeting to Hell.'

'Those are not the terms that I would use.'

'They're the terms that getup represents.'

'This "getup," as you call it, represents a lot of things, of which the Bible and its teachings are important parts. But not everyone of Faith accepts the Gospel as the literal Word of God. Many Catholics, no less devout, appreciate the Word as metaphor. Therein lies its greatest beauty, and its everlasting relevance, since each of us must answer for him or herself the questions of existence. So when you speak of Heaven and Hell, I have to look within, knowing that the meanings at which I arrive may differ from those embraced by former times and cultures, or even by my peers. Faith is not a static institution, Julian. It has to breathe. And breathing, it is subject to the rule by which all life proves it "*is*"—the rule of change.'

'I think you're an odd duck, Ms. Zoë.'

'That may be true. So, give me your interpretation.'

'All right. When a man puts his fist through a mirror, he cuts his hand.'

She had to laugh. His matter-of-factness undercut her sermon. There was, however, no denying the gravity of his conduct. He had attacked himself. A mock suicide, to be sure, but a definite warning that Julian's thoughts were once more self-destructive.

'My tribulations must be particularly comical today. You're the second person I've had laughing.'

'I really shouldn't be. It is rather serious, you know.'

'Merely a superficial wound. "Maimed" was for effect.'

'It was to the act itself I was referring.'

'Ah well, look at it this way: during a fleeting twinge of inner-loathing, mistaking a facsimile, the patient hauled off and slugged himself, whereupon the illusion shattered, leaving the original unscathed—relatively—to ponder fate's ironic sense of humor. Like it?'

'No. You're avoiding the…'

'How about: his life in a shambles at his feet—actually at my waist, since the glass fell into the sink—he realized that Man was far less fragile than his image?'

'I wish you would use that mind of yours for something more productive than repartee.'

'Oh? I thought that second one was pretty close to your ego vs. essence theory—the I of my I survives.'

'The difference is one of conviction. You don't believe the things you say.'

'Now she shows her colors! Faith makes truth. The moon *is* made of cheese.'

'You leap before you look, Julian. If you're truly interested in understanding, don't criticize so perfunctorily. Of course believing a thing does not make it true, just as disbelieving a truth does not make it false. The point is, you have an exaggerated skepticism, and that won't lead any closer to the truth than would credulity. Of what are you afraid?'

'"Of what"—don't you ever end in prepositions? Of losing, Ms. Zoë, my life, for instance. Like everybody else, I'm afraid of dying.'

'Then why are you pursuing death so hotly?'

Snatching his jacket, he jumped to his feet and stomped across the room, then turned to face her.

'You call that therapy!?'

He exited, slamming the door behind him.

* * *

Julian's door was open when Sister Dana arrived. The room was set as for a class, chairs placed at the table, chessboard out replete with pieces, though in a rather sparse configuration, and in whose midst there stood a piece of paper folded tent-like—a note that the nun, bending sideways, tried to read.

'Boo!'

'Oh! Oh, Melanie, it's you.'

The student scanned her teacher's tidy room, noting Julian's absence as well as his missing snapshots.

'Where is he?'

'I don't know. Not here.'

'What's that?'

'A note, I think.'

'For me?'

'I couldn't see.'

Melanie plucked it up and read:

1. Jz2 JtelephonesQ
2. JxQ or QxJ
3. Jj2:15?

———————

1. Mj2 SDj2

White to move and mate in three

2. Mj2:15 SDxM
3. (MxJ rescheduled)

'What does all that mean?'

She looked back and forth from the paper to the board.

'It's chess notation. But the letters are funny.'

She thought a moment longer.

'Oh.'

'What?'

'I get it now.'

'Well?'

'Julian went to Sister Zoë's at two o'clock to make a phone call.'

'His mother, I'll bet.'

'His mother?'

'When she heard he was missing she wanted to come. Sister advised her not to, but I guess she's coming anyway.'

'Why isn't she here then?'

'The roads have been closed, remember?'

'Hm. Well, here he calls her the Queen.'

She paused, wondering at the JxQ or QxJ.

'What? What?'

'Well, he may be back by 2:15. I'm supposed to work on this problem until then, and if he hasn't shown up, you and I can leave. He'll reschedule my class another time.'

'You got all of that from that?'

Melanie smiled, self-satisfied, and tucked the note into a pocket of her jeans.

'Want to be Black?'

'What? Oh, no thank you. You know I can't play.'

Melanie sat down at the board, and soon was lost in concentration, leaving Sister Dana free to inspect the room.

Orderliness reigned. The nun thought it phony. Julian did not live this way, she was sure of it. The neatness was a put-on, a mask like all his other masks, which hid, she was convinced, a cruel, conniving, sexually perverted male—a wolf in sheep's clothing. She smirked at the metaphor's aptness. If only there was a way, she very much would like to see him leave the sanitarium. For good. But how? And did she have the right to plot against him? He was, after all, a patient who had come to them for aid. Sister Zoë had taken him in (though she believed the reverse was true, that he had taken in Sister Zoë—taken in everybody except herself). Why, really, had he come?

Since her avowed reform, the nun had asked herself, repeatedly, what the Lord intended via Julian. Was he a sort of test? He had certainly occasioned her to do some soul-searching. And perhaps, without his base example, she never would have seen the error of her ways. Perhaps God's plan was that she fall from grace temporarily, just so she could recognize, in Julian, absolute wickedness. In fact, how better to forge a shield for Melanie?

There must be something here that would incriminate him, a lever she could work (if his mother failed to come). Yet the room, done up as it was, appeared almost unoccupied. She saw then that the bathroom door was closed. She opened it and slipped inside unnoticed— Melanie still intent on solving the chess problem.

But the bathroom, too, was immaculate. Laid out neatly on a towel were: a toothbrush, tube of toothpaste, can of shaving cream and a disposable razor, deodorant, tweezers, nail clippers, a brush with a nylon comb. On the rim of the tub was a bottle of shampoo. She checked the wastebasket. It was full of broken glass. Then she saw that the door of the medicine chest had jagged shards of mirror wedged along its frame. That explained his hand. She clicked it open: aspirin, eye drops, baby powder, and a box of prophylactics. She checked to see if any of the tinfoil packets were missing. Too bad; all there.

'Sister Dana?'

'Just a minute.'

She flushed the toilet, waited, then went back out.

'Do you have a pen?'

She took one from her habit.

'Any paper?'

'No, not with me.' She looked around. 'Do you think there might be some in one of his dresser drawers?' She crossed to see.

Melanie panicked. Julian's photographs! What if they were there? She especially did not want the nun to see that nude. She wanted no one to see it, ever. She remembered the note.

'Never mind! I'll just use this.'

Disappointed, the nun returned. Melanie tore off an unused portion of Julian's instructions.

'You solved it?'

'Uh huh. Nothing to it.'

She lettered out the problem's answer, including variations, then added in the improvised notation:

1. Mm2:20 Jm?
2. MxJ JxM

thus expressing her idea of offering him a drawing as partial payment for the lessons. She propped her cryptic note between a pair of pawns.

'What should we do now?'

'I think I'll go back to my room. I have some makeup work to do in Math and English.'

'Want some help?'

'No thanks. The Math is real easy. For English I have to write another boring composition.'

'That's an odd assignment, "write another boring composition."'

Melanie smiled. The nun did, too. Closing his bedroom door, they took their leave.

* * *

He would simply have to tell her he was not ready to leave. That should be easy enough. Regardless of what he had told Ms. Zoë, he always got his way—unless it did not matter. This, however, mattered—mattered deeply; it was absolutely essential he finish The Game.

But what could he tell Mother Dear to keep her at a distance?

And should they talk in private or should Ms. Zoë be present?

His earlier tantrum, no doubt, had gotten the old nun worried; she had confirmed his morbid state. How, then, to use that as a means for gaining time—time to work on Melanie?

Julian plotted as he walked. The snow compacted underfoot. Upon reaching the nun's quarters, he heard the chapel bell toll twice. He knocked and entered.

'Punctual as usual.'

'I said I'd be here. Here I am.'

'You still sound angry, Julian. Are you?'

'Yes. I'm missing Melanie's lesson.'

'Oh, I am sorry. I had forgotten, or I would have suggested another…'

'Skip it. Let's get this over with, shall we?'

Sister Zoë retreated behind her desk, picked up the telephone and dialed.

'Mrs. Philomena Papp, please…'

'No. It's Sister Zoë. Your son's here with me, though.

Just a second, I'll put him on.'

She offered Julian the receiver.

He did not hesitate. In fact, he veritably snatched the phone from her hand.

('Hello, Mother Dear. I'm fine. Don't come. Goodbye.')

He clamped his hand over the mouthpiece and spoke to the nun.

'Always keep things short and sweet, do Mother and I... She's now protesting that I'm cruel... and that after having traveled all this way...'

He stopped to glower at Sister Zoë.

'Where is she?'

'Payson.'

'Where the hell is that?'

'Julian, talk to your mother. When she heard that you were missing...'

('Right. Sorry, mom. Sister Judas has just informed me that you're practically in town. Payson is it?... Fifty, sixty miles away... Hm, hm. "Goddamn snow."') His hand again covered the mouthpiece. 'She's frantic about my quoting her within your hearing.'

'Would you like some privacy?'

'No, no. I'll edit.' He addressed his mother. ('Ms. Zoë will hear an expurgated version from here on out. So, what's up?')

He listened quietly for a moment.

If only the nun could see his eyes, but with his glasses on—and with his usual deadpan expression—his face proved unreadable. She would have to depend on scraps he tossed her, and on their conversation afterward.

'She's expressing doubts, now, about your competence, Ms. Zoë. She's in a bit of a snit about my "sabbatical." Should I bail you out?'

('No, Mother. The fault was mine not hers.')

He grinned sardonically.

('I took a walk, was all. Got lost. It started to snow. I found a cabin. What's to tell; I rode out the storm in style; the place had *all* the creature comforts.')

The nun had expected as much, and wondered at Julian's withholding this account. She watched him closely, aware more than ever before of the chess player's machinations.

'Oh, oh. She's asking about my seizures. Treacherous footing here, Ms. Zoë.'

('Yes, Mother. I cannot tell a lie; I've had one recently. Again, my fault. I've been remiss in popping the pills. They give me nightmares—or so I thought. Ms. Zoë has been trying to convince me to the contrary.')

'She wants to speak to you when we're finished, Ms. Zoë. Don't forget how generous I have been.'

('Yes, Mother… Yes, Mother.')

Sister Zoë felt a pang of guilt. Julian was drawing her into his own conspiracy. He was enjoying himself; it was obvious. Why? Because Julian, it was apparent, had total control.

Then suddenly he changed. He turned aside as he spoke. His tone grew less abrasive.

('She's just a patient here.')

('No, she's just a kid. Amnesia victim.')

('Yes, she's pretty—if you're into baldness and pedophilia.')

('As a bat. A little fuzz is all.')

('I didn't say. None of us know. I'd guess thirteen. What is this? Drop it.')

'I'm getting the third degree about Melanie.'

('Listen, Ma. I think you'd better go back home.')

('That's right, without your baby boy.')

('I know you're close, but I've been feeling kind of down.')

('All right… All right… But not before. Okay?')

('Fine. I'll tell her.')

'Mother Dear wants to wait it out, in case I change my mind when the roads are finally cleared. I said okay.'

'Okay with you?'

Sister Zoë considered. It would buy a little more time.

'Okay with me. Agreed.'

('I have to go now, Mom. Goodbye.')

He held out the phone. Sister Zoë could hear Philomena talking to the air.

'I leave it to you, Ms. Zoë, to corroborate my misgivings. If you'll excuse me?'

'Julian, wait.' She took up the phone. 'Mrs. Papp, this is Sister Zoë again. Hold on.'

But Julian was already out the door, hurrying back to his pupil.

Upon returning to his room, he found the note from Melanie:

"MxJ and JxM"—now that should prove an interesting exchange.

* * *

Some people say that no matter what happens to a person, in some way it is always that person's fault. I have been thinking about this. I do not think it is always true. Sometimes accidents happen. A person might walk out into the street and get hit by a car. Maybe that person wasn't looking. If the car comes and kills a person because the driver wasn't looking, though, it might not matter if the person was being careful or not. In that case, it's dumb to say that the person got run over because she wanted to.

This is another example. Suppose a man is a thief. He wants money fast. Maybe he is walking down a crowded sidewalk in a city. He sees women. So he chooses one and snatches her purse. Is that the woman's fault, just because she got picked? No. She couldn't help it.

A lot of things happen that people can't help. You can say it's good luck or bad luck, but still, it's just chance. Bad people can have good luck and good people can have bad luck. So when something bad happens to a good person, it isn't always that person's fault.

She counted... 201. Mrs. Soames had said 250 to 300 words.

And to blame people themselves for the accidents or crimes or illnesses that happen to happen to them, is wrong. Julian Papp didn't want to get seizures. I didn't want to get raped.

She stared at the word—raped. She felt it punch her in the stomach, make her sick, make her fight for breath. Was it true? The word had no concrete associations, merely sense memories that ached dully—like cold in mended bones. She dropped the pen and clasped her hands, squeezing them hard between her legs, her shoulders hunching, her body rocking, waiting for the insect sounds to swarm into her ears. She braced herself, heart pounding, drumming loudly like fists on a hollow wooden door.

The door! Sounds were coming from the door.

'Come in!'

Julian appeared. Her rocking halted. Instantly the madness left her eyes, her fears retreating.

'Are you all right?'

After taking a deep breath Melanie found she was remarkably composed. The insect sounds had not invaded. The word was there on the page. And now she knew. Not in a comprehensive way; specifics still lay hidden. But cognizance—of what her mind so desperately had feared—at last had dawned.

'Yes, Julian. I'm all right.'

He looked relieved. She noticed. He tried to camouflage his concern.

'That's good. It's no use teaching chess moves to a zombie. Memories astir?'

He tried to peek at her composition. She turned it over.

'None of your business.'

'Let me guess.'

'No!'

He knew something. She was not sure what that was, but did not want him telling.

'Suit yourself. So, what exactly did you have in mind?'

He nonchalantly strode about, pausing to inspect her sparse belongings. Everything, of course, had been provided by the nuns, principally Sister Dana: clothes, some toiletries, her sketchbook and drawing materials, her Bible, a digital clock. Though the room was physically much like his, atmospherically it was feminine. Turning back, he caught her in a blush.

'Bet I'm the first man ever to visit your room.'

'So what!'

She had blushed from anger. She disliked his trying to pry into her things.

Alerted by her tone, Julian changed strategy.

'Only here for your lesson, of course. Can't have you missing two in a row. Or would you rather make it up another time?'

She did not answer immediately. She wanted him to leave and also to stay. She wanted to be hugged and left alone. And most of all she felt she wanted Julian to understand.

He finally caught a sense of her confusion.

'Another time, then. I'm sorry I bothered you.'

He retreated to the door.

'Wait! Don't go.'

She had to talk to someone. Of course, she could scarcely tell him that. Still, the lesson could be her excuse. She cleared the desk off, then repositioned it between the bed and chair. He came back to help. Together, they set up the board.

'I thought we'd play a game out loud this time.'

She looked puzzled.

'I mean, we'll talk it through. Every time I make a move, I'll tell you what I have in mind. You do the same.'

'But if I have to tell you what I'm thinking, then I'll lose.'

'The object is to learn, not to win.'

He said this rather pointedly.

'Sorry.'

'You play White, okay? Begin.'

She pushed forward her King's pawn two squares.

'Well?'

'I don't know. You do it.'

'That's hardly a viable reason.'

She frowned.

'It opens paths for both the King's Bishop and the Queen.'

'And seeks to control?'

'The center.'

'Good. That's better.'

He replied with his own King's pawn, stating similar

reasons. She slid her Bishop to c4.

'What are you thinking with that?'

She kept her eyes lowered.

'I'm thinking I want to talk to you about something.'

They both were aware of levels being shifted.

'Something you remembered?'

She nodded.

'About a black van with a fisheye window?'

It felt as if the floor had dropped from under her. Her eyes winced shut. She saw it—the van, its headlights glaring, parked beside a tree with greenish skin. She pulled back, drawing further and further away, until the scene at last was swallowed up by darkness.

Wide-eyed now, she gazed at Julian, taken aback.

'How?'

'I don't know. A dream.'

'About me? You had a dream about me?'

Before that moment, Julian had not realized how comforting his doubts had been. But knowing now that this image held meaning for Melanie, his nightmare took on insupportable dimensions—which he felt less prepared to bear then she.

'It was only a dream. Nothing to take too seriously. Relax.'

Her hands were clenched. She hid them in her lap.

'Maybe it was only a dream to you, but not to me. It happened. There were three of them.'

Again she started at her own disclosure. Things were coming back too fast: faces, voices, smells, terrible sensations, excruciating pain, and then the insects whining, screaming incessantly until she…

Julian watched the terror as it overwhelmed Melanie's body, saw her shoulders stiffen, her forearms cross, her fingers clutch her shirtsleeves, saw her face become a writhing, agonized mask. She tried to fight it. He felt powerless. He could not help her—though he tried, he rushed beside her, hugging her tightly in order to suppress her awful trembling, hoping to add his strength to hers to arrest the impending screech. It came nonetheless… collapsing her will… eclipsing mind and soul with its brutal energy… building… burning… detonating under Julian's bandaged hand.

He hardly realized that he had grabbed her. The outcry, now over, left her alarmingly limp. The floor was strewn with fallen chessmen and Julian's overturned chair.

Now what?

'Melanie? Melanie!'

She was insensate, catatonic. Her eyes were blank, her mouth agape. And there was blood. Whose, hers? No, his; his injured palm was a gory mess.

He picked her up and carried her to the bed. He used his knee to ease her down. He arranged her limbs to make her body look more natural, then wondered why. Was he trying to help or was he attempting to cover his tracks, pretend it had not happened, protect his selfish interest in The Game's continuation?

Finally it struck him, as he stared at the result of his pseudo-psychoanalyst's tampering; this was not a pawn, but a human being.

He reached his hand toward Melanie's blood-smeared cheek and touched it tenderly.

'I'm sorry, Melanie.'

He backed away, then left the room as it was.

* * *

Julian did not report the incident. Instead, he holed up in the library, where he was wont to go whenever he needed a place to think.

He used a desk and chair in a far corner rarely occupied by anyone other than himself, tucked away as it was on the second floor with scant light and no window.

He had memories, too. Maybe not so horrific as Melanie's. But they were his. And some were ugly. And he recalled them:

an episode in elementary school, Halloween, kids and costumes, at a party where a classmate came wearing clown-white makeup, sunglasses, and a bleached-blond wig...

another elementary school incident (before children's cruelty to freaks and outcasts grew subtler), his glasses snatched off in the cloakroom, "say cheese," his defenseless eyes nearly blinded by a camera's flash...

then there was the time in junior high, when a film clip of "Albinism in Nature" was shifted, all in "fun," from the screen to Julian's clothes, a polar bear pup projected onto his shirtfront.

Childhood pranks, insensitivities, tasteless jokes; he had run the gamut. Was it any wonder that epilepsy had delivered the final blow?

"Grand mal memories" he dubbed them in retrospect— a misnomer in the sense that his seizures caused awareness of themselves to be erased. Nevertheless there persisted numerous impressions of intense humiliation, the most enduring of which took place at the last match he had played.

It was repercussions from that which had prompted his overdose. He had tried a second time in the hospital, but that attempt, too, had failed. Thanks to Mother.

Mother Dear—his pal, his champion. Mother Dear— his lifelong friend; without his mother he would be dead and buried—twice.

Instead? He was sitting in a dusky library at a half-assed sanitarium playing hypothetical chess with an old-maid nun.

Julian examined his hand. The blood had dried and turned brown. The gauze was sticky at the edges. He pried one loose. He sneaked a peek. Five stitches had torn. A flesh wound, merely. He put the gauze back in place. Flesh wounds heal.

But what about the other wounds, the non-corporeal kind, the injuries to one's psyche and self-esteem? Like his? Like Melanie's? When did injuries like hers begin to heal?

When she admitted them. When she faced up to the fact that a gang of sadists had assaulted her, and the fault for this was *theirs*, not hers in the least. She *must* remember. And he could help her. He had proved as much with the detail from his dream—which was the trigger to her relapse, he was sure.

The light had grown so faint that Julian himself seemed to be its source, his white clothes glowing under an isolated wing of bookshelf shadows. He failed to notice. His concentration no longer wavered; it had a focal point, a goal. A fresh line of play had reopened, as well as a reason to sustain his very life.

* * *

Sins. There were so many of which the nun was guilty, did she dare to ask for favors beyond her Lord's forgiveness? But the proximity of Julian's mother—so close and yet so very far—had inspired Sister Dana to humble herself and feverishly pray.

'*Please* let her come and take him. *Please* let her come and take him.'

She had been lying prostrate before the chapel's altar for three-quarters of an hour, maybe more. She checked her watch. Melanie's Bible class was at seven. It was now 6:55. She would have to hurry. She got to her feet, rubbed her arms and the fronts of her thighs, then diffidently genuflected.

With a last impassioned plea in her eyes, she gazed up at her Savior. Then she turned to brave the bitter-cold outside.

The wind was stiff. It blew her habit into billowing pitch-black wings that flapped and beat along her ribs as if enraged at flightlessness. The expression on her face—a grimace—grew fixed. Tears streamed from her eyes. Her gloveless hands curled into fists against the chill. She broke toward shelter.

At Melanie's door Sister Dana paused to blow her

nose. Her face felt frozen. She worked her jaw to restore some circulation. Then she knocked.

No answer.

Dinner hour was over; the girl should be back from the cafeteria.

She knocked again, then opened the door to look inside.

The room was dark. She made her way to the lamp. Something snapped underfoot and she started. She groped for the light, and in its flash beheld the scene.

'Melanie?'

The girl lay just as Julian had left her—eyes vacant, limbs arranged in a sleeplike pose. Blood still smeared her mouth. On seeing it the nun went wild with concern.

'Melanie!'

She rushed to check for vital signs. Thank God; the girl was breathing. She dabbed at the blood. No cuts? No scratches? She could find no wounds of any kind.

Julian! She must have bitten him in self-defense; when he attacked her. There had been a struggle; that was clear. The room was a shambles. All the bedclothes were rumpled. And Melanie's clothes? Fearfully the nun explored for evidence—zippers, buttons. All were fastened; the clothes were simply disheveled. Relieved, she gently stroked the victim's scalp.

'Poor baby. Poor baby. What did he do to you? Did he hurt you? Are you Marcy again, my love?'

The nun was crying. It was so unfair. How could God be cruel to those so innocent? She nearly cursed a faith that taught, "God's Will is perfect." But she resisted. And, instead, she knelt to pray.

'Dear Lord, oh Father, help me understand. Help my Marcy. Whatever she has done to deserve such punishment, please forgive her. Or punish me in her place. And certainly punish him—Julian Papp. Make him suffer, Lord, *eternally* for what he has done!'

She gasped, abhorred by what she had just invoked.

'I'm sorry, Lord. I... Forgive me? Forgive him, too? Oh God in Heaven, please forgive us all!'

She wrapped the covers around the girl, leaned forward, kissed her lightly on the cheek, and left to carry the urgent word to Sister Zoë.

* * *

Julian finally returned to his room, falling wearily into bed. Throughout the evening, flashbacks of Melanie's relapse had plagued him. "He should not have left her." There was nothing he could have done—nothing anyone could have done; the girl, in time, would come around—or so he hoped. Still, his mind kept repeating, "he should not have left her."

Then there was the scream itself, and Melanie's effort to contain it. He had felt it overpower her, irrepressibly—like one of his seizures.

He felt it even now, as he laid his head against the pillow, hearing his own pulse, feeling it throb through his body as hers had throbbed when he held her in his arms, tightly, trying to help… He *had* tried to help… He honestly had.

The tape, goddamnit. Gimme some fuckin' tape!

Help!

Jesus fucking Christ, shut her up, will ya? How in hell am I supposed to drive?

Shit! She bit me.

Help!

Slug her.

Bitch!

You wormy little chicken-shit. Get off yer candyass an' help me hold 'er. Fuck! Goddamnit.

You'll kill her.

I will if she lifts that knee again. Hear that, cunt? Hear me?

Stan! Really, you're gonna kill her hittin' so hard.

Not yet, I'm not. Eh, Elmo? Not yet? Fuck! Aren't you even man enough to pin two scrawny ankles down?

I've got 'em, I've got 'em! Stop hittin' her!

We're gonna do a lot worse, Pauly. Right, Elmo?

Yup.

Slap another strip of tape across 'er yap, Pauly, an' roll 'er over. Let's have a look.

She's passed out.

Has she? Good. Scissors.

What?

Scissors. Hand me the fuckin' scissors. Maybe if we cut a flap in the seat of 'er pants, Elmo will drive a little faster.

Fuck off.

We outta town yet, Elmo?

I'll tell you.

You do that, Elmo, you just do that. And I'll tell you what we got us here... Pink panties, Elmo. And whataya know? Pink backside, too... Say 'ah'... Oooooo, Elmo! Wait'll ya see this asshole—tight as a sailor's pocket. You'll need a fuckin' crowbar just to pick it. Get it, Pauly? Pick 'er pocket? Wanna see?

No. I don't feel so good.

You get sick and I'll pinch yer cocksuckin' head off.

Elmo, you better pull over.

Fuck off. Jesus fucking Christ. Here. Hurry up! Why do you keep draggin' along these amateurs, Stan? Watch the carpet!

Wanna throw him out with his puke?

We oughta. We really oughta. Is he through?

Sorry, you guys. Go ahead, Elmo. I'll be all right now.

Christ.

Hey, where the fuck are we?

Keep your shirt on.

Sure, Elmo. Mine stays, hers goes. A bra, Pauly. No bra. Shit, man, nice pair, eh? Tug those blue jeans off 'er.

I can't. The tape's in the way.

You taped her legs together? God, what an asshole. Hey, Elmo, this idiot taped the cunt's legs together. Why not tape yer pecker to yer balls? Or here, better yet, snip the mother off. Elmo, hand me my razor.

Get it yourself.

Prep 'er, Pauly. Get 'er pants pulled off an' spread 'er. Stan the Beaver-Barber's on his way. Pretty good, eh Elmo? Stan the...

I've heard it.

Stan! Stan!

What?

She's not breathin'!

Sure she is. Look at 'er tits. Pauly, if I'da known you was such a pansy, I'da never let ya come along. Now gimme back them scissors.

She's hurt bad. Look at her hand.

You did that, for Chrissake, yankin' 'er through the fuckin' door.

I didn't do anything!

No?... Well, suit yerself. Hey, Elmo, I guess you get her ass an' snatch. Pauly's pud's a pollywog... Man, look what you're gonna miss. Look at them firm little titties all round an' new. Don't they make ya wanna suck 'em? I'll bet she's got 'er cherry, too... Christ, she has! Looky here; I can hardly get my pinky in. Elmo, she's a virgin!

Her bunghole's mine.

That's what I like about you, Elmo, ya know exactly what ya want in life. Wait'll ya see him do 'er, Pauly. He busts 'em like a fuckin' jackhammer. Hand me that pillowcase an' crawl back down to 'er feet. Maybe you can whack off between 'er toes. As for me, I got some scalpin' to do. God almighty, curls galore! Ain't it wonderful, the way she's cooperatin'?

She's bleedin'.

Where?

Under the tape. It'll choke her.

Hmm.

Maybe you should take it off.

And have the cunt screamin' bloody murder again?

She's out cold.

Not for long. Elmo never fucks 'em 'less they're wide awake. Ain't that right, Elmo?

What?

That you wan'em conscious when they get it?

Yup.

He says the more it hurts, the more their little assholes squeeze. You'll see.

She's really havin' trouble breathin'.

Almost through. Razor time! Never leave a solitary hair—except for eyebrows. You can come up here an' give 'er mouth-to-mouth when I do 'er snatch. We there yet, Elmo?

I'm lookin' for a place to pull over.

Here, Pauly, wanna do 'er pits? Run it up an' down 'er legs? No?... Switch places then. If she comes to while you're peelin' off that tape, tell 'er one peep an' we gut 'er.

Hang on back there.

What the fuck you doin', Elmo!

Found a dirt road.

Well, go easy, will ya? I'm collectin' fur—what little there is. That's the trouble with jailbait; their muffs'll hardly stuff a matchbox.

Her lip's split.

Teach 'er not to bite. She'll have to learn soon.

Are you really gonna make her blow you, Stan?

Make her? Pauly, by the time this cunt gets 'er gums on me, she'll be beggin' for it. You'll see... I do nice work, don't I? Any place I missed? And get yer fuckin' meathooks off 'er tits. You already forfeited yer share.

Since when?

Ha! I knew it! Hey, Elmo, nurse Pauly here's finally gotta hard-on. Was it feelin' up 'er titties, Pauly, or watchin' her twat get plucked? Should we give him sloppy seconds after all, Elmo?

We're here.

Hallelujah! Just a once-over on her arms an' shanks an', presto—clean as a fuckin' whistle. We're ready when you are, Elmo. Elmo gets first crack. Get it? First crack?

Wake her up.

What about Pauly, Elmo?

After. Maybe.

Hear that, Pauly?

She's still out.

Shake up a beer and give her a squirt.

Thar she blows!

Watch it, shithead, you're drippin' on the carpet.

Sorry, Elmo. Slap 'er, Pauly.

She's comin' around.

Bend her over.

Here we go. Will ya look at that pig-sticker! Lord have mercy; she'll be squealin' for dear life. You'll never get it in 'er, Elmo, not with all the goose-grease in the world.

Hold her. Tight.

We got 'er, Elmo, we got 'er.

Uhhhhh!

Shut yer face, bitch.

No. Let her holler.

Okay, Elmo... Jesus to God she took 'im! Go, Elmo, go!

Uhhhhh! Uh! Uh! Uh! Uhhhhh!

It's the heat rub, Pauly; sets their assholes on fire. Go, Elmo, ride 'er, bang 'er, hump, hump, hump 'er.

Uhhhhh!

Whew, that was fuckin' fantastic, Elmo. I'm surprised ya didn't bust clear through. That's one asshole that'll never be the same.

Keep that towel under her.

Where's he goin'?

For a walk. Elmo never watches once he's through. She's all ours! You first, Pauly.

No, you go ahead.

Shriveled up again, eh? Does yer mother know you're a fag?

I am not a fag.

You've got fresh pussy right under yer fuckin' nose an' ya can't even get it up? That's fag shit, man.

Butt-fuckin's what's queer.

Oh, oh, oh; you better hope to God Elmo never hears what you just said or you'll be gaggin' on yer own two balls. I'm not kiddin', believe me… So, you gonna bust 'er cherry, or do I have to show ya how?

She's passed out again.

Here.

No. I want her this way.

To each his own. Heave ho.

Do you have to watch?

Afraid ya don't measure up?… Okay, for Chrissake, I'll turn my head. Get on with it. Elmo ain't gonna wait around all night… What the fuck are you doin'?

You said you wouldn't watch.

Are you kissin' 'er? Is that what you're doin'? Jesus Christ, what a moron.

Shut up, Stan. Shut your goddamn mouth!

Okay, okay. I'm not lookin'. Go ahead, Lancelot. Get it? Lance a lot?

I guess ya got it. Go, man, go. You in? You in? Pump

'er, Pauly! Let 'er have it! Cream the fuckin' bitch! Wake up, you miserable cunt. Come on, open yer eyes. Show some appreciation for what you're gettin'.

Here, Pauly, wipe with this. You did 'er. Look. You did 'er real good.

Please.

Did she say somethin', Stan?

She said "please". I told ya she'd be beggin' me for it. Come on, darlin', up on yer knees. Ya got one more hole needs pluggin'. Now say 'ah,' an' don't lemme once feel any of those teeth or I'll knock 'em down yer fuckin' throat... That's it... Tongue an' lips... Sucky, sucky... a little faster... Sucky, sucky. Oooooo, that's nice. Ya do that real... FUCK! GODDAMNIT! PAULY, HELP ME! PULL 'ER OFF! NO! MAKE 'ER LET GO! JESUS, GOD, HELP ME! BITCH! BITCH! BITCH!... Oh my God, oh my God, oh my fuckin' God!

Did her teeth go through?

Oh my fuckin' God. Bitch!

Stan. Stan, did her teeth go through?

I don't know. I'll kill 'er! I swear I'm gonna kill 'er!

Let me see.

Is it bad, is it bad? Pauly, tell me it isn't bad.

She bit it off, Stan.

WHAT! Don't tell me that, you motherfucker!

She did. The head. I'm sorry. It's bleedin' bad.

Oh my fuckin' God. Jesus Christ. Get Elmo. Elmo! You guys gotta get me to a hospital. ELMO! Pauly, where's the scissors? Where's the fuckin' scissors?

I don't know.

Tape 'er, Pauly. FUCK!

But Stan...

Do it, goddamn you!... Mouth, too... Now light me a cigarette.

You wanna smoke?

Don't argue with me!

Here. Here, Stan.

Now go get Elmo. And HURRY!

Bitch, bitch, bitch, bitch, bitch, bitch, bitch, bitch, bitch, bitch, bitch, bitch.

Stan, what're you doin'!

I'm burnin' fuckin' holes in this cunt's corpse. Bitch, bitch, bitch, bitch.

You killed her?

I will.

Dump her, Pauly.

Where, Elmo?

In the wash. Get movin'.

Hey! Hey! Where you goin' with that bitch? HEY!

Stan. Stan, let him go.

I'm not through with 'er.

Stan. Stan!

Pauly, where are you? Where the fuck are you, ya cocksucker? PAULY!

Stan.

Where is she?

Stan, she's dead.

What?

She's dead, Stan.

Pauly, you sure?

I checked, Elmo. I'm sure.

Then let's get the hell outta here!

No, I wanna smash 'er face.

Into the van, come on!

Smash 'er.

Pauly, ya got him in?

Yeah, yeah, GO!

Smash 'er… smash 'er fuckin' face… smash 'er.

The headlights ceased to cast their sallow beams across the cactus. The silhouettes of brutish men were gone. The desert night reclaimed itself, black, then midnight-blue, then gray, its tattered shadows faintly pooled beneath a waning moon. The landscape almost sighed as peace prevailed, a threat-less calm… and yet the scene was somehow incomplete.

Her eyes adjusting, Melanie explored the dimly lit tableau.

The van?

No.

The men?

No.

Me?

Unfolding like the petals of a once-forbidden flower, Benjamin's gnarled fingers slowly opened. There, upon his fate-scored palm, a huddled figure lay. Bald and bloodied, battered and bound, its form, in miniature, was the embodiment of pain. Terror deformed its face. So much so, that Melanie at first refused to recognize it. But Benjamin was patient. His hand awaited, trembling with that pulse which seemed to animate his carvings, offering the truth. It was she, in every sad detail—her eyes and nose and cheeks and chin, her naked limbs, her frame. She lay pathetically contorted... but nonetheless alive.

May I hold her?

She cupped her hands. The miniature touched her palms. It was warm, yet made her shiver.

It really happened?

He nodded gravely.

Why?

His words would not allay her trickling tears; already she was weeping.

You wrote it in your essay. Chance. Life, we all must learn, is good *and* bad, unjust *and* fair; without its contradictions, Life lacks meaning.

She stroked the tiny replica. Its delicate proportions seemed to breathe.

And I'm still...?

Living, yes.

Through watery eyes she again surveyed the scene. In the wash she found the spot where she had lain. Tenderly she placed her double there, by a creosote bush, on drought-cracked earth, not far from a green-skinned tree.

And my name is Melanie?

Melanie Chamberlain, yes.

* * *

Unlike before, Julian strove to expel the horrors of his dream. But the imagery endured. He remembered everything, as if his mind, like film, had caught the action frame by frame, and then, upon his waking, played it back—repeatedly—until the gruesome details burned in his brain like firebrands.

* * *

From the window, bundled in her quilt, Melanie had watched the dawn—or appeared to have watched, for it was impossible to tell what her staring eyes perceived. Her lips had moved from time to time, mutely mouthing words, which the nun found pointless to decipher. So, while the girl sat motionless, Sister Dana had tended to everyday chores: drawn a bath, made the bed, taken clean clothes and laid them out on a chair.

Suddenly, Melanie stirred. Her hand worked free from the quilt, her finger pointed at the frozen pane, touched it, and with slow, deliberate strokes began to letter out her name—first... and last.

The nun looked on as though she were witnessing a miracle, continued looking, as the letters bled then ran into squiggly streams.

'Melanie Chamberlain.'

She read the name aloud as if intoning Scripture. Was this the sign for which they all had prayed?

'Melanie?'

Eyes still devoid of outward focus, the girl withdrew her hand.

'No? Not yet, my sweet?'

The letters' ghosts re-fogged with steam. In spite of herself, the nun was glad. More time. More time together, sharing quietly the joys of loving care and need.

Sister Zoë would have to be informed, of course. But not until young Mr. Papp was safely on his way. If Melanie indeed showed progress, once she came around, it would never do for *him* to be anywhere in sight. This time Julian's interference was not to go unpunished. The chess player's speedy departure, in fact, looked assured.

She led the unresisting girl from the window.

'A nice warm bath is what you need, my darling.'

They went into the bathroom.

'Stand still; I'll undress you. There, my precious. Careful now. How beautiful you are. Relax, lie back, and let me soothe your sorrows.'

Trying to sort through Sister Dana's account, with all its inferences and accusations, had been difficult. The facts were that Melanie had relapsed and that it was highly likely Julian was involved. How, was the question. Sister Zoë did not believe Sister Dana's attack-and-run scenario, although she did suspect that a clash of sorts had occurred.

Why had he not come to her? If Julian had been present when Melanie slipped back into stupor, why had he not come forth with the information? Unless he was responsible. Or unless he was afraid that he would be blamed. Which, of course, he had been. And he must have known he would be, having made no attempt to cover up his guilt.

Round and round went the explanations. Only Melanie and Julian knew the truth.

Speak of the devil.

Sister Zoë curtailed her ruminations to watch Julian cross the common. It was early. Perhaps her gamble to wait, give him a chance to come on his own, was about to pay off. She moved from the window to the door in anticipation of his knock. She was rewarded. She let him in, noting immediately how altered he appeared.

His face showed stress. His cheeks looked gaunter.

She sensed that his glasses hid a troubled gaze. He seated himself in front of her without uttering a word.

'Would you care for some tea?'

He shook his head.

'Or some coffee? I could have a pot sent over.'

'I didn't come for stimulants, Ms. Zoë.'

'No, I thought not.'

'How is she?'

'As you left her. Would you like to tell me how it happened?'

'I touched a nerve, she threw a fit, I tried to calm her down, she fainted… or got spaced-out or whatever you call it—catatonic.'

'What do you think triggered it?'

So she was asking for his opinion, finally. Quickly he shifted from the defense to the attack.

'You're the shrink. You figure it out.'

'Are we playing our little chess game again?'

'Very good, Ms. Zoë. You've figured it out. But it is *I* who hold the key to Melanie's cure.'

'And thus you challenge my authority. Would you prefer that I step aside? All right. In the spirit of the game, then, state your case.'

Her move was a surprise. Julian had expected condemnation for his meddling. He had almost hoped for it as a relief from his self-reproach. This open invitation to espouse his private theory was a welcome, yet intimidating, offer—to be accepted with caution.

'I've had another nightmare... That's not accurate. I've had my *recurrent* nightmare. Same one. Only this time I remember it completely. I know exactly what you're thinking—"not this again; how could Julian's dream-life have anything to do with anyone but himself." And I'd be the first to admit it couldn't. Except, Ms. Zoë, this nightmare isn't mine; it's Melanie's.

'Now, before you have me fitted for a straightjacket, let me explain. I've tested it out. Melanie is in the state she's in because a detail I supplied to her jogged her memory. But she couldn't face it. She tried; I could feel her trying. It's just too strong for her to handle. If you'd seen what I saw, in the dream, you'd understand. Real animals, these guys were—the ones who put her in that hospital before she was sent here. Yes; I've read her file. I sneaked a peek at it one morning when you weren't here. All's fair in love and chess. I confess to the deed now so you can appreciate the fact that *nowhere* in that medical report is there any mention of a van with a fisheye window—the detail that sent our patient back to The Land of Nod.

'Of course at the time I was more concerned about proving my theory than about Melanie's welfare, so I blew it. I fed her too much too soon. But next time, when...'

'Excuse me, Julian. Do you really think it's fair that Melanie should have to suffer through your teaching yourself psychotherapy? As you say, you've already made a mistake. Who is at risk if you should make another? Now I'm quite prepared to listen if you'd care to describe your nightmare, but I cannot condone, nor will I permit, your tampering with my patient.'

'How possessive of you, Ms. Zoë.'

'No—how professionally responsible.'

They had reached an impasse.

'May I see her?'

Sister Zoë was pensive; she still had doubts about Julian's motives. The relevance of these nightmares—irrespective of their accuracy—was that they represented a curious sort of link, one patient to the other, both of whom were impressionable and imaginative. Thus their affecting one another indeed was plausible. What remained a mystery to the nun was how. And where, in the end, would it lead? Did she dare risk another setback? In the girl's present state, could Julian's going to see her do further harm?

'Yes, you may.'

He got up to go. She stopped him.

'Provided you are willing to give me assurances that there will be no more playing doctor on your part. Agreed?'

He nodded.

'No more games, Julian. They do a great disservice to you both.'

For once he did not care about The Game.

She let him leave.

* * *

Julian had run. He paused in the hallway outside Melanie's room to catch his breath. He leaned against the door and watched his glasses fog with steam. He took them off. He decided to leave them off since the light inside was tolerable.

He knocked.

Then it occurred to him that the girl might be attended… though no one came.

He grasped the doorknob, turned it silently. He stepped inside and froze. Melanie was there. She was sitting by the window calmly, placidly. She did not stir.

Julian closed the door behind him—again as soundlessly as possible—and took up a position at the foot of her bed. He could see three-fourths of her face from where he sat. He watched; she stared.

The light, as it fell on her immutable expression, lent her skin an almost opalescent luster, quite incongruous, since it belied the awful blankness in Melanie's eyes.

She looked estranged, though her gaze was tranquil. She appeared to be at peace, yet Julian found her state decidedly offensive. The spark that once ignited the girl's intelligence was doubtlessly out.

He grew impatient.

It was boring, this insentience. He wanted to shake her, to wake her up. He wanted to apologize for his callousness, make amends. But how could he? He fumbled for his glasses. They fell to the floor.

A familiar sensation then gripped him. His thumbs began to twitch, his eyelids to flutter.

wind breathing soft gentle meadowscents and meadowcolors walking (touch me touch me) passing through the air molecules of air pulsebeat footfall time adrift (she)...

Melanie suddenly turned in her chair (like a magnet to its pole) and looked, with a fleeting recognition, at Julian's face.

The door opened.

'You! Out!'

Sister Dana rushed between them, mantling Melanie's body with her outstretched shawl.

'You've done enough already, Mister Julian Papp. Leave us alone. Get out. Get out!'

Julian, stunned and disoriented, staggered as he stood. The meadow? Melanie? Sister Dana? He escaped the room, careening down the hallway as he ran.

Without his glasses Julian's flight to the woods was a torturous ordeal. He literally groped his way, using his hand as a sunshield, often falling. He slowed his pace.

Had he experienced his aura without a seizure? Yes... except it was different; Melanie was there. Which seemed impossible. Yet he had seen her. And she had seen him.

He spun around and headed back.

He *had* to talk to her—immediately—while things were vivid in his mind, while he still could envision his meadow with Melanie in it.

How much time had elapsed since he had stood where he now was standing, Julian could not tell. He knocked, barely waited, then barged in—to an empty room. His spontaneous momentum stalled and died. He felt defeated. He felt exposed. An utter fool.

Despondent, he sat down on the bed. What was he doing there? Who was he trying to confront—some spacey, frog-haired teenager—or himself? And what had he to do with this "child" in the first place?

Nothing. Absolutely nothing. He had "dreamed", was all, merely suffered a nightmare—which seemed to have *some* basis in reality. So what? He seemed to have an affinity for this girl—but only as an element in The Game—which was likewise imaginary, of course, a mere invention on his part to pass the time, to stave off the boredom of an everyday grown chronically inane. He thought about the schizophrenic games he had played at the cabin, how danger lay in losing one's objectivity. Was that what he had done? Had he acted rashly? Should he sweep his arm across the board and start afresh. Or would it not be better simply to resign?

He looked around at Melanie's room, glad she was not there. Still catatonic, she could only serve to remind him of his blunder. Except she *had* surfaced—for a moment, anyway. He was certain she had recognized him. And he had seen, or sensed… what? His meadow? Had she really been there? After, or before, or was it during? No— impossible. Auras were "the preambles of seizures", mere "symptoms" of a condition known as epilepsy. The facts were irrefutable. Why persist in doubting them? What foolish impulse made him think, even for a second, that his meadow could be shared with someone else?

He saw his glasses. Sister Dana must have found them, for they were now on the dresser. He got up to retrieve them. They lay on a book—the kind that has nothing but empty pages bound inside. He opened its cover and idly read, My name is Marcy. I don't know how I got here but here I am. With a twinge of interest in the unfinished Game, he mentally reexamined its position. If a winning move was to be found, he needed more evidence. Without a qualm, he stuffed the journal under his jacket. He crossed to the door, checked the hallway—all clear—and quickly left.

Chances for a clear-cut win looked a little more promising.

Anticipating Julian would come back for his dark glasses, Sister Dana had taken Melanie for a nice long stroll. She had seen the look the two had exchanged. She had not understood it, but it had scared her. Whatever influence Julian had was stronger than her own. The girl had nearly torn away, nearly risen from her trance, as though abducted by some vile, perverse seducer. But she had acted quickly and her ward was safe and sound—though as they reentered Melanie's room the girl behaved strangely.

'Not again.'

'What, Marcy?'

'How long has it been this time?'

'What, since we left for our walk?'

Melanie tried to think. She could never seem to reconstruct the order, as if like playing cards, her memories all got shuffled. She knew she had paid a visit to the Miniature Man—a rather long one. And Julian was prominent, before maybe, or after. Not much else was clear.

'Take off your coat, my sweet. Lie down and rest.'

The nun could sense her patient struggling to recall. Would she remember her name, the surname she had written on the windowpane? Certainly, supplied with that, the authorities could trace her. Parents would be found. They would come. And Melanie would go away… forever. The nun hung up their coats inside the closet. Melanie sprawled on the bed.

'Oh!'

'What?'

'Julian.'

'What about him?'

She sat back up.

'He was in here just before I screamed.'

The essay sprang to mind. She checked her desk.

'Did you see a piece of notebook paper anywhere? It had a composition written on it.'

'I put all your school things in that drawer.'

Melanie pulled open the top left drawer.

'Find it?'

The last word veritably jumped up from the page. She read: "raped"—smelled it, tasted it, knew its horrid sights and sounds and sensations—and, finally, she accepted it as true.

Bit by bit more details rematerialized: Julian telling her about his dream; the image that matched her own; the van; the wash; the terrifying faces of that brutalizing night; and Benjamin—protecting her from the traumas of her past.

The plastic chess set rested on her desktop. A pawn lay broken. Beside it lay a tiny tube of glue. Sister Dana moved behind the girl, sensing her reverie's import. She braced her patient's shoulders with nervous hands.

'I'm sorry about the chess piece, sweet. I stepped on it by accident. I meant to mend it. See, Marcy?'

Melanie picked up the tube of glue. She opened it and squeezed. Had Benjamin called her by her christened name? A dollop oozed out. He had. She pressed the pieces of the broken pawn together. Melanie… something. Slowly, like a photograph developing before her eyes, the memory of who she was appeared.

She set the pawn back on the board and turned to face Sister Dana.

'Why do you keep calling me Marcy?'

The nun faltered.

'I… hadn't realized. Have I been?'

Melanie suddenly remembered that not only had she heard her name, she had written it. Where? On the window, in the frost, in Sister Dana's presence.

'What's my name?'

The question was more like a challenge. It had the tone of an accusation.

'It's Melanie. I forgot, that's all. Marcy—Melanie, the

names are very sim…'

'I mean, my last name.'

There was no mistaking her tone now; Melanie was bristling with indignation. The poisoned pawn. The warning. Sister Dana.

'But, Marcy, I…'

'Melanie. My name is Melanie. Melanie Chamberlain! And you knew it! And you didn't tell me!'

'Melanie, I'm sorry. I didn't—I wanted—I mean, I wasn't sure that you were ready. I wanted to…'

'You wanted to keep me here forever. For yourself!'

'Oh, no! I love you!'

She tried to soothe the girl, to hug her. But Melanie squirmed from her embrace and backed away, her eyes keen with mistrust.

The nun felt stabbed by Melanie's look, impaled. She dropped to her knees. She bowed her head, unable to face her beloved's outrage.

'Please forgive me!' She began to sob. Her body trembled. She was abject in her suffering. 'Please don't hate me, Melanie. Don't hate me; I couldn't bear it.'

Her sobs redoubled.

Melanie, repelled at first by Sister Dana's vehemence, grew embarrassed, then compassionate. As the poor nun's tears continued, she took a step toward her.

'I don't hate you, Sister Dana.'

'Yes you do. And I deserve it. I've been selfish, and it's

true; I wanted you to stay here, Melanie. I wanted you to be my friend.'

The girl stepped closer. She reached her hand toward the kneeling woman, touched her wimple.

'But we are friends.'

The nun looked up at her.

'Do you mean that you forgive me?'

Her eyes implored with such humility that Melanie again found herself embarrassed.

'Uh huh. Sure I do.'

Sister Dana exhaled with a peculiar little whimper. She got to her feet. She kept her head bowed, trying to avoid the young girl's eyes.

'May I… May I hold you?'

Melanie stiffened slightly, but did not shy away; this the nun interpreted as consent. Tentatively, then firmly, she gave the girl a grateful squeeze.

'You are a saint, Melanie. Thank you.'

They parted. Melanie moved to her dresser—relieved that she and the nun would still be friends—and excited that this very day—Wednesday, November 12th, at 9:15 A.M.—could mark the last and final entry in her journal.

She rummaged through her things.

'What are you looking for?'

'My journal.'

'It's on your… It was, I mean.'

'Where?'

'On top of your dresser. I set it there myself.'

'Well it isn't here now.'

'I see that. And neither are Julian's glasses!'

* * *

The library had preserved its sepulchral silence. Julian took his contraband to an isolated nook and settled down for an hour of surreptitious reading. He did not plunge right in, however. In fact, he kept the "borrowed" journal closed. There was something not quite right about his stratagem.

* * *

After Sister Dana's elucidation of "the facts" with regard to her journal, Melanie was persuaded that Julian had taken it. She did recall his visit (albeit hazily). She recalled many, many things, and, as her recollections accelerated, the alleged theft (temporarily) dwindled in significance. Before long she and Sister Dana were racing, in an enthusiastic whirl, toward Sister Zoë's quarters.

The elder nun, of course, was overjoyed—though she tempered her outward response with an inward reservation. This apparently complete recovery was a most encouraging turn of events. The girl, however, could yet be prone to setbacks. Certain gaps in memory might persist.

Sister Zoë considered it prudent to secure essential data first, while the opportunity lasted.

In their excitement, the missing journal might easily have been ignored, but at its mention Sister Zoë was quick to see its import. She exchanged some words, aside, with Sister Dana, who was then dispatched. This had seemed fortuitous, affording as it did the chance to interview Melanie alone without neglecting Julian (about whom the nun was legitimately worried). So, under an injunction to "be tactful and considerate," Sister Dana rushed to fetch Mr. Papp.

The cheek of it, the unabashed nerve of stealing from a helpless girl, stealing something as sacred as a diary, incensed the young nun. It was cowardly. It was mean. And it was typical. She was almost glad. This, most certainly, would be the final straw. Yet Melanie, alas, would go away; that was now inevitable. But at least the girl's tormentor would have been scourged. She would see to that! If only she could nab the fiend red-handed—though

Sister Zoë had simply said, "Find him. No accusations; we have no real proof he has taken it. Just send him to me." But so obvious was his guilt—especially if she found him wearing his glasses—that it was unimaginable he would have the gall to deny it.

She climbed the stairs to Julian's room. Without knocking she bolted in. He was not there. She made a rapid search. But the journal was not among his things. She found his photographs, however. Filth! She pocketed the one of Mercedes. She marched into the bathroom and confiscated his box of prophylactics. Evidence was mounting. Now, if only she could prove, in addition to his sexual depravity, that Julian Papp was also a lowdown thief! She left his room and hastened from the dormitory.

Where next? He was not in the rec. room; she had passed that way en route. Perhaps the cafeteria. The rock salt crunched beneath his stalwart step. Patient or no, Julian must be punished. This catering to his "suicidal tendencies" was absurd. It was time he faced reality, took responsibility for his malicious acts, and suffered the consequences. What if Melanie had not recovered? What if his attack had caused irreparable damage? Why Sister Zoë had tolerated all he had done she could not fathom. The man, the "boy," was unquestionably a menace.

He was not in the cafeteria. "Where doth the devil's

loathsome serpent coil?" She clenched her fists and headed toward the library.

At the sound of footsteps Julian calmly exchanged the journal for a look-alike book, then waited. Soon he heard a throat being cleared behind him. He closed his finger between some pages and turned. The nun fell for the bait. In triumph, she snatched the counterfeit from his hands.

'Sister wants to see you, Thief.'

She glowered at his dark glasses.

'Interested in existentialism, are you?'

'What?'

He grinned as she opened the book. She slammed it closed.

'Where is it?'

He answered by turning up his palm to accept the book's return. His smugness maddened the nun still further. She wanted to slap his ghastly face. She clutched the crucifix of her rosary to subdue her temper.

'We know you stole it. You're evil, Julian. Evil.'

'So have me excommunicated.'

Casually, he pretended to resume his reading.

'Sister meant right now!'

He turned again.

'Listen, you.' He paused—resolved that the "poisoned pawn" would lure no takers. 'Go tell Ms. Zoë—and use these very words—that Julian says he'll come when he's fucking ready.'

She could not stand it. He had seen right through her, and what was worse, he had not even deigned to answer her heated charge. Had she stayed a fraction longer she would have strangled him—or would have tried to. In a rage, she turned, and stormed off down the aisle.

* * *

Sister Zoë, reviewing the salient points of name, address, and phone number, put aside her notes to marvel humbly at the human mind's resilience. It seemed her patient had, indeed, recovered. Wounds still were present (which only time and love would heal), but the spiritual essence of Melanie Chamberlain had survived. Sister Zoë gave thanks... then added an impassioned prayer that her next decision would not rescind this blessing.

Sister Dana knocked and entered, her features still distorted by her wrath.

'I see you found him.'

'I found him all right, skulking in a corner of the library like a criminal!'

'And he refused to come.'

'He certainly did!… How did you know?'

'Come over here to me.'

She obeyed. Sister Zoë took the upturned face and cradled it in sympathetic palms, smoothing the furrowed brow, coaxing out the tension, stroking, soothing, coddling, until the ugly signs of hatred all but vanished.

'There now, isn't that better? You must try to keep your beauty free from such unsightly masks.'

'Yes, Sister.'

The wrinkled hands still held her. They felt a blush flood through the younger nun's cheeks. The elder placed a kiss on each and smiled.

'Before we talk of Mr. Papp I want to say how pleased I am about your work with the young Miss Chamberlain.'

Having been obsessed with the emotions raised by Julian, Sister Dana failed to notice that Melanie was gone. Now she did—with great concern.

'Where…?'

'I sent her off to get some lunch. She doesn't remember breakfast.'

'Oh no! She isn't better, then? Totally, I mean?'

'Don't fret; her memory is quite restored. Just little things still give her trouble. Normal things, though. I'm sure the worst is past. And in large part, she has you to thank.'

'I did very little, Sister. Nothing, really.'

'Nothing? Don't be silly. You gave the most therapeutic

gift of all, Sister Dana. You gave your love. That's what sees us through such times. I have watched you very closely, Sister. This has all been quite a trial for you. I even had some doubts about your pulling through. But every time you weakened, I believe Our Lord lent you strength. You have discovered from this what love is, and, maybe more importantly, what it is not. You will learn much more. So, as far as Melanie is concerned, I'm very proud of you.'

Were these things true? To her shame the younger nun could only recognize her lapses—all those times her efforts to keep the Faith had failed. She could scarcely believe that she merited anything but censure. And yet there was a reassuring voice inside. She had changed. She had been touched by something good and right and pure.

'Julian, however, is another matter. Come, sit down.' They sat close to each other on the couch. 'You have not done well with him thus far.'

'Because I hate him, Sister. Oh, I know how awful that must sound, but I can't help it. Julian's evil.'

'He is *ill*. And you *can* help it. And you *will*. The root of what you found to love in Melanie exists in everyone— even in Julian; though I admit it is better hidden. In fact, he has buried it so deeply he makes one doubt it's really there. But I assure you, Sister, it is. And reaching him is every bit as crucial as it was for Melanie. Do you understand that?'

'Yes, Sister.'

'Good… So, with that in mind, tell me what he said.'

'I can't.'

'You what?'

'I can't repeat it.'

'His words won't reflect on you, Sister Dana. Go ahead; you have my permission.'

'He said to tell you that, "he'll come when he's fucking ready."'

'Oh dear. He did?'

'I'm sorry, Sister. I didn't want to say it, but you…'

Sister Dana stopped abruptly, thoroughly bewildered. Sister Zoë was laughing. Then, without knowing why, she was laughing, too.

'Those were…?'

'His words exactly, Sister. I'm sorry.'

They laughed some more. The old nun finally dried her eyes.

'Well, as I said, it's buried deeply. Did he have the journal?'

'Not with him. I'm positive he stole it, Sister. Though I can't imagine why, except he's such a…'

'Yes?'

'Such a sick person.'

'Yes. He is that. He is also much, much more. And it might be wise to keep in mind that Julian—no less than we—has a genuine interest in Melanie's recovery.'

'In *her*, maybe. Not in her recovery.'

'No, I think you are mistaken. I think, in some peculiar way, her health has been the object of his game.'

'What game?'

'The chess game based on who could cure the girl's amnesia first—Julian or I. His mother gave me insight into that. I knew, and yet I didn't know. Does that make any sense?'

'I couldn't say, Sister. What are you going to do?'

'He has put me in a difficult position. With this latest bit of impudence, he has challenged my authority. Did you tell him anything about Melanie?'

'No.'

'So he doesn't know… though he might have guessed. Why else would he force this confrontation?'

'You're asking me?'

'No, I guess I'm asking myself. He is going to have to see the girl.'

'Oh, no, Sister! How could you even consider it? What if he does something awful? What if he makes her forget again? Think about Melanie, Sister, please! It isn't right to risk it, especially for the likes of him. Here, look.'

She exposed the contents of her pockets, holding them up for Sister Zoë's inspection.

'Where on earth…?'

'His room.'

'You didn't! Sister, you know very well, "staff does not

make searches of patients' rooms." This is quite a serious offense.'

'But you're not seeing what's important. He's depraved, Sister Zoë. Just look. Do you want a person like this to undo all…'

'Sister Dana, enough! It is not up to us to judge. He has had the decency, at least, to keep these private. Would that you had done the same.'

'But…'

'We are going to step aside and let them meet.'

'Sister, no!'

'You are not to interfere.'

The young nun knew it was wasted breath to argue any further. Still, she could not help from rendering her opinion.

'I pray I'm wrong, but I think you're making a terrible mistake.'

'Pray I'm right, Sister Dana; it's much more positive. Pray hard. And let us dearly hope our Good Lord hears.'

* * *

The cold bit cruelly as Julian strode across the common.

He ignored it. The match, the Royal Game, had taken precedence again—its outcome imminent. He knew this next move was likely to be the last—if only he could steel himself to see it. No seizures now. His senses must stay absolutely clear. The pills! His step faltered. Had he taken them?... Yes, swilled down with his morning coffee. His brisk pace resumed.

Melanie, having returned from lunch, was going through her drawings. She had them carefully arranged—her farewell gifts—all around the room: Sisters Zoë, Dana, Deborah, and Morgan, Mrs. Lowry, Mrs. Soames, and Mr. Jimmy, her six self-portraits crowned by various coiffures, the sketches of Julian in all of his guises, and finally Benjamin—the Miniature Man—Benjamin, her long-lost friend.

Odd that he had come back into her life. He had owned a shop beneath their old apartment in the city, before she and her family had moved away. The hours the two of them had spent together, the wondrous fun! All her fondest childhood memories seemed drawn from times with him—dear, sweet, gruff, old Benjamin. Then one morning he was gone—died in his sleep, her parents told her—though, at the time, she found their explanation unconvincing. For Benjamin had promised her that he would be her friend for always. 'For always never ends or dies,' he had said.

'So you've revived.'

She spun around.

'Julian!'

He was standing in the doorway staring. Her first reaction was to cover up her work. But that was useless; he had already seen. In fact, he stood right beside the drawings she had done of him. She might as well just let him look, let him choose his present for himself.

Then she saw what he was holding.

'Hey, that's mine!'

She rushed to reclaim her journal.

'Here.'

He gave it back.

'How could you!'

'Easy—you weren't here.'

'And so you stole it?'

'Borrowed. I haven't even read it.'

'Ha, I'll bet.'

She turned the pages, as if scanning them for his fingerprints.

Meanwhile, he continued his sidelong appraisal; she seemed strange. Something in her nature betrayed a subtle alteration. What? A sketch arrested his attention before he could decide.

'This is wonderful.'

Melanie stopped her fussing.

'What is?'

'You're quite good.'

Stunned, and not a little flattered, she put aside her journal to join him, as he made a pensive tour about the room. His focus was divided—half directed to the work, half to its creator. He paused.

'Who's this?'

'That's Benjamin. You don't know him.'

He studied her closely.

'Hm. The gatekeeper?'

'Who?'

'The what-did-you-call-him, the Miniature Man?'

'Uh huh.'

She seemed unfazed. He *had* read her journal, every last word of it—just as he had memorized her file. More than that, the dream had taught him (in unsettlingly grim detail) about the rape. And toward his own ends, he had used it, used it all, regardless of its impact on this girl— whose gaze was now a mirror for his... whose mind, at last, had shed its austere guard... whose heart was opening, reaching out, inching closer, closer, closer. Mentally Julian wrenched away; physically he did not move. The portraits on all sides seemed to hold him prisoner. From the corner of his shielded eyes he watched their faces watching... mute indictments... The Game, his precious Game, the crime of which he stood accused.

Then, eerily, the charcoaled lips began to mouth reproofs:

Julian.

Julian?

J u l i a a a a a n.

The portraits called, each voice a breathy whisper.

You're very clever, Mr. Papp. But are you bright?

You're evil, Julian. Evil.

What gives you the right to yell at me?

Of what are you afraid?

… evil, Julian. Evil.

People who make fun of other people are just covering up for what they don't like in themselves.

Don't let conceit deprive you of a helping hand; we all can use one every now and then.

… evil, Julian. Evil.

I'll beat you at this game some day.

You'll never beat me, Marcy.

Why *do* you want to end your life?

You'll never beat me…

… evil…

The smears of black and white increased their contrast—blacker, whiter—then formed ranks, straight rows of alternating squares. Figures crept from left and right and took up their positions, as Pawns, Rooks, Bishops, Queens, and the rival Kings—the Knights stood clear, as did six Pawns, four white, two black—the early casualties—expendable—in a contest wherein victory was all that mattered. The seconds ticked. The board revolved… upon its pedestal… above the void… an empty plane... or a plateau that stretched to infinity... or rather to the horizon—sun-bleached, shimmering, vaguely visible in the distance, not so distant, drawing near, revealing earth and grass and tree and leaf and cloudless sky... *wind breathing soft gentle meadowscents and meadowcolors walking (touch me touch me) passing through the air molecules of air pulsebeat footfall time adrift (Melanie) yes (touch me hold my hand) the meadow smiling as we walking floating reaching touch to touching palm to palm two palm prints pressing lines whose fates conjoined inscribe the way so clear so clear so clear*

Of course.

If Qxg3 then Bf6 mate. Otherwise, White captures the hapless Queen.

'The Game is won; Black has no choice. Zoë must resign!'

The girl looked puzzled.

'Julian? What are you talking about?... Julian?'

His mind returned.

'Let go; that hurts.'

The two were standing face to face, and (at Julian's instigation) hand in hand.

'Where is that place?'

She had not released him. He stopped resisting.

'Place?'

'That meadow.'

It now was Julian's turn to look puzzled. His aura?

Shared? He shut his eyes... *meadowscents and meadowcolors walking (touch me touch me)...*

She lifted his glasses. His eyes stayed closed. He spoke.

'You're there.' His eyes opened. 'And you're here... And I'm not shaking from a seizure or my aura?... You're actually here?'

She pressed his hand to her cheek.

'Yes, Julian. I always have been.'

He staggered back. She did not, could not know the implications—'the only *un*-lonely place I've ever known... a presence... feminine... something I carry with me when I go back to the game... beyond even winning.' Winning. The Game! His hand broke contact. He had seen the move. Would it pass the test? Had he really won, or was the girl's recovery merely temporary?

Melanie sensed his shift in mood and grew wary. His eyes suddenly looked ruthless. She tried to reestablish contact, reaching for his hand again. He veered.

And then she winced in anticipation as Julian lowered his dark glasses.

'Stan. Pauly. Elmo.'

He spit the names. She saw the rapists. The insect sounds arose... then swarmed...

But Melanie withstood their shrill attack.

Then she slapped Julian, very hard, across the face.

* * *

The slap still ringing in Julian's ears, he proceeded to Sister Zoë. He had won. He had won!; the nun was certain to acknowledge it. Why hadn't Melanie?

Not that it mattered. She had her memory back. She would be okay, when she simmered down. Of course she despised him for rubbing her nose in the truth, but such was life. He had played the heavy intentionally. He had been harsh—maybe a little callous. He had been mean, in fact. He had overdone it. Why?

Because *she* had trespassed on his territory, showed him that his meadow was accessible, filled the space so perfectly he could close his eyes and see her, as if the presence in his "aura"—feminine but kindred—had been Melanie's (or someone like hers) all along?

What had she said—'I always have been'—when he had wondered at her being there? Was it any less likely that she had shared his meadow than he had shared her nightmare? More importantly, had his refuge been restored? And had it returned to him as reliably as the past had returned to Melanie?

The snow was beginning to melt as Julian's sneakers stamped their imprint. Despite his regrets about how things were left with the girl, his step was confident, self-assured. The Game was over. His play had been inspired. And he had won.

Upon hearing his knock, Sister Zoë bade Julian enter. Once again he seemed changed. For the better? His posture was certainly more erect, his stride more energetic as he crossed to her desk, stopped, and waited—or, rather, loomed with an air of expectancy.

'I take it you have seen our patient, Mr. Papp.' (At her using the pronoun "our," Julian smiled.) 'It went well?'

'Well enough. She has recovered. A tad ungratefully.'

'Oh? You quarreled?'

'Let's just say she chose a peculiar way of thanking me.'

'But she's…'

'Nothing to worry about, Ms. Zoë. Melanie's fine. Though I admit I was a little rough… Nonetheless, she survived it intact—even feistily.'

His bravado seemed a trifle too contrived.

'And you, Julian? What about you?'

'What about me? Well, that's why I'm here; I should have thought it was obvious.'

She scrutinized him carefully, his straight aggressive stance, his hauteur, his superior aspect. Was he cured? Was his ego—which she found so objectionable—revivified? Was he invulnerable—hence insufferable—once again? Or had this game he had been playing (superimposing on them all) accomplished something more than Julian's merely chalking up another win?

He was waiting, armor refurbished... (Would she concede? Would she understand?)... refurbished but somehow altered, perhaps, underneath.

With a slow, deliberate motion Sister Zoë reached for the telephone, and, lifting the receiver, resignedly dialed.

* * *

Wednesday, November 12th, at 6:15 in the P.M. I'm going home! Everything has happened. I talked to both my parents on the phone. I was so happy I cried. They did, too. They said they loved me and that was all that counted.

I can hardly wait until tomorrow. That's when they'll be here. Tomorrow! Everyone is very pleased, even Sister Dana. I thought she'd maybe make it hard for me to say goodbye but she's been wonderful. So has Sister Zoë. I'll miss them. I'll miss everybody.

I'm all packed. There's nothing more to do. I've given out my presents even. Except for Julian's. That part's sad. He's gone. His mother came and got him. I was watching from my window as they drove away.

I hit him. I feel terrible when I think about it. He made me remember. I don't know how, exactly. It was all a little strange. He had these nightmares and I was in them, and I had daydreams that he was in, too. How he got there with me, or I got there with him, I don't think I could tell. But he's the one who made it clear to me just who it is I am, though he was nasty about it like he always is when he thinks that someone likes him. And now he's gone. I'll never be able to thank him or tell him that I'm sorry. After Benjamin, Julian's the best friend I ever had. And I didn't even know it.

This will be the last page of my journal. I'm keeping it along with some drawings and with Sister Dana's Bible and Julian's chess set, which he left for me with Sister Zoë. I'm going to remember this place, and especially Julian, for always. Just like Benjamin said, for always never ends or dies.

ACKNOWLEDGMENTS

Bobby Fischer (White) vs. Dr. Reuben Fine (Black)
New York, 1963

WHITE	BLACK
1. e4	e5
2. Nf3	Nc6
3. Bc4	Bc5
4. b4	Bxb4
5. c3	Ba5
6. d4	exd4
7. 0 – 0	dxc3
8. Qb3	Qe7
9. Nxc3	Nf6?
10. Nd5!	Nxd5
11. exd5	Ne5
12. Nxe5	Qxe5
13. Bb2	Qg5
14. h4!	Qxh4
15. Bxg7	Rg8
16. Rfe1+	Kd8
17. Qg3!	Resigns

We hope you enjoyed *The Miniature Man*.
Would you like to know about some of our other books?
Visit www.snowbooks.com for details.
Small Publisher of the Year 2006